The princess Finnglas is in the deadly grip of the evil Sea Monster, deep down in the mysterious underwater realm of the Sea Witch. And Niall has been bewitched by the mermaids.

Pangur Bán, the white cat, is desperate. He must rescue them—but how can he free them from enchantment?

Only Arthmael can do it. But who is Arthmael? Where is he? Can Pangur find him in time?

Fay Sampson is the author of nine books for children and teenagers. She lives with her family in a centuries-old Devon cottage, overlooking Dartmoor. As well as writing, she works as a part-time teacher of mathematics. She spends her holidays collecting material for her books—anything from sailing the Hebrides to learning to drive horses.

To my God-daughter
Anne Perry

Pangur Bán
the white cat

FAY SAMPSON

Illustrated by Kathy Wyatt

A LION PAPERBACK

Published by
Lion Publishing plc
Icknield Way, Tring, Herts, England
ISBN 0 85648 580 2
Lion Publishing Corporation
10885 Textile Road, Ypsilanti, Michigan 48197, USA
ISBN 0 85648 580 2
Albatross Books
PO Box 320, Sutherland, NSW 2232, Australia
ISBN 0 86760 477 8

First edition 1983

The verses from 'The Student and His White Cat'
from *Poems and Translations* by Robin Fowler are reprinted
by kind permission of Constable and Co. Ltd.

Printed and bound in Great Britain by
Cox and Wyman, Reading

Preface

In the Dark Ages monks and nuns were great travellers. So were their cats. We know because they wrote about them – in the margins of their beautiful hand-copied Bible-books and in the journals they kept. One monk, leaving Ireland, wrote: 'I think I shall take the little cat with me.' Another, more sadly: 'The white cat has gone astray from me.'

Far away in a monastery in Austria, the notebook of an Irish monk came to rest. For centuries the book lay undisturbed. There was no one in the monastery now who could read the Irish language. Then, more than a thousand years after it had been written, someone picked up the dusty book and opened it. Hidden within its pages he found this secret poem:

> I and Pangur Bán, my cat,
> 'Tis a like task we are at;
> Hunting mice is his delight,
> Hunting words I sit all night.
>
> Oftentimes a mouse will stray
> In the hero Pangur's way;
> Oftentimes my keen thought set
> Takes a meaning in its net.
>
> 'Gainst the wall he sets his eye
> Full and fierce and sharp and sly;
> 'Gainst the wall of knowledge I
> All my little wisdom try.
>
> When a mouse darts from its den,
> O how glad is Pangur then!
> O what gladness do I prove
> When I solve the doubts I love!
>
> Practice every day has made
> Pangur perfect in his trade:
> I get wisdom day and night
> Turning darkness into light.

Verses from *The Student and His White Cat*

NOTE: Bán means 'white' and is pronounced with a long 'a' as in 'barn'.

1

The white cat, Pangur Bán, was a killer. He crouched and waited.

There was definitely a mouse in the hole. He could see two bright, black eyes watching from the darkness.

The cat's white claws were tucked out of sight beneath him, but he was not resting. He lay low and still on the floor, but he was not asleep. Under his half-closed eyelids a narrow line of green showed, pierced by a black slit. He was watching. Every muscle was stretched tight, like a bent bow-string, an instrument of death.

'Don't move,' said Niall the monk, 'or I'll murder you.'

Pangur Bán did not answer, though he could talk very well when he wanted to.

Behind him, in the dusty sunlight, the long room was full of murmuring sound. Monks and nuns were bending over books, copying. As they traced the words, they said them aloud, so that they hummed over the painted pages, like brown bees in a meadow of flowers.

Where the open door gave on the sea, and the light fell brightest, young Niall sat painting the great title page of his Gospel. Three years he had been working on it, and there was no artist like him in all Erin. He was a giant of a man, an oak-tree. But his strong brown hands could trace patterns as delicate as a spider weaving a cobweb on an April morning, and then paint them with all the splendour of the hills in autumn.

The calfskin page in front of him was stabbed with compass points. Red ink-dots, like drops of blood, traced the pattern. Ribbons of purple and blue twined between them, coiling, curling, circling. Knots of gold ended alarmingly in serpents' heads. And beyond their scarlet tongues, silver chariot wheels spun and spiralled upwards, till the whole rich carpet of the page became a letter p, flanked by astonished angels.

Now only one little empty space was left on the ivory-white vellum. In less than an hour it would all be finished. Niall flexed his tired hands and looked up. His gaze fixed on Pangur, and he dipped his pen carefully into the scarlet paint. In the last corner of the page he began to outline with tiny red dots the shape of a white, crouching cat.

And the mouse came out of its hole.

Pangur Bán sprang.

With a squeal, the mouse was away. Under benches, under tables, under desks, to the far, dark, dusty end of the room. And Pangur Bán went after it, claws bared. Over the sandals of the monks, under the skirts of the nuns. The sound of their reading turned to shrieks of alarm.

The mouse reached the wall. In a panic it turned and swarmed up the white robe of the nearest nun on to her desk.

Pangur Bán whirled round, white feet in the black dust, and tore after it. Now they were flying back down the room over the table-tops. Dirty paw-prints on every clean white page. Claws tearing the painted words as he sprang. Pots of ink flying through the air. Shouts, cries, anger.

The mouse made a last leap for the sunlit doorway. Pangur Bán pounced on to Niall's desk. The pot of paint flew from the monk's hand, tipped over the all-but-finished page and rolled to the edge of the table. A pool of scarlet flowed out of it and began to drip, drip, drip on to the floor.

Pangur leaped after the mouse.

And Niall blocked the doorway. He was in a towering fury. He seized a stool by one leg, like a club. As Pangur skidded to a halt, Niall raised it above his head. Pangur sprang sideways. The blow smashed on to the floor. It would have split his skull.

'Help!' cried Pangur. 'Save me!'

Again Niall raised the stool.

'You murdering vermin! Look what you've done to my

Gospel! Three years' work you've ruined. I'll dash your brains out for this!'

Pangur cowered.

'No!' cried a brave voice behind him.

Martin pushed in front of Niall. He was the youngest of all the monks, newly-come. A prince, who could have been king when his father Kernac died. But he worked in the kitchen. At night he fed Pangur with bread and milk, then held him purring on his knee. Now he was as white as the milk itself, and not a quarter the size of Niall.

But, 'No, Niall!' he cried again. 'Don't hit him!'

'Out of my way!' roared Niall.

The stool crashed down again. And Martin threw himself under it, shielding Pangur.

He went down like a felled ash tree and lay in a heap on the floor. He was whiter than ever. Blood was trickling down the side of his face. The shouting was suddenly still.

'Martin!' cried Niall, kneeling down beside him. 'Martin! I didn't mean to! Not you!'

Pangur Bán crawled back into the shadows under the table and hid behind the skirts of the nuns.

Martin lay very still. The trickle of blood faltered and stopped. Behind him, the scarlet paint was still dripping off the table. Plop. Plop. Plop. It was the only sound in the long room.

The old nun Ita came forward. She rubbed a pewter paint pot against her sleeve. She held the shining metal to Martin's mouth. When she took it away, there was not a cloud of breath upon it. She looked at Niall and her face wrinkled in grief.

Donal the monk knelt down and felt for Martin's heart. No one spoke. At last he took his hand away and looked at Niall. They were all looking at Niall. And then they looked at Pangur.

'Martin?' mewed the cat.

'He's dead,' said Donal.

And there was only the sound of the waves swinging against the cliff. The monks and the nuns were all looking at Niall and Pangur.

Outside the door, the mouse scampered away in the sunshine. Safe.

2

Drusticc the Abbess stood on the beach, slender and white-robed on the white sand. She was young, loved and feared. They had buried Martin that morning, under the sea-pinks on the cliff.

'Now go!' she cried, her voice strong as the herring-gull's.

Niall knelt before her on the beach.

'But I didn't mean to kill him! I loved the lad. It wasn't my fault! It was that devil of a cat!'

Over his head her voice stormed. 'Of course it was your fault! Was it Pangur's hand that lifted the stool? Was it Pangur's arm that held it over your head? Was it Pangur's shoulders that brought it crashing down on Martin's skull? How could you do it, Niall? Martin, whom all of us loved. Martin, who never did you any wrong. How can you say it was the cat?'

'But he spilt the paint over my beautiful Gospel! He tore the page! He trampled his filthy footprints over everything!'

Pangur shrank further under the boat where he was crouching. There were no shadows dark enough to hide a white cat. He knew that it was true. Martin had died for him. He saw it in the faces of everyone he met. If they had not been monks and nuns they would have kicked him as he passed. No one fed him bread and milk now. No hand reached down to stroke his head.

Two monks came staggering down the beach. One carried a sack. The other had a cask on his shoulder.

'Go!' cried Drusticc in a ringing voice. 'Here is food and water. Go, until a year and a day have passed, and the spring has come to Erin again. And hear the penance that I lay upon the pair of you for the blood you have spilt.'

Pangur pricked up his ears and listened. Over his head was the swish, swish, swish of a brush. Enoch, the convent's fisherman, had been building the leather curragh all winter. Bending the wood, sewing the ox-hides, stepping the mast, cutting the sails. It was almost finished. Now he was painting it with hot sheep's grease to make it waterproof.

'You shall take a boat and go wherever the wind of God shall carry you. And wherever you go, you shall redeem with the lives of others the blood you have spilt; one life for every drop.'

Niall clasped his hands pleadingly.

'But I'm afraid of the sea! I can't sail a boat! I haven't *got* a boat!

'It is that or death. There is a boat behind you.'

The pot of grease smacked into the sand beside Pangur. The sticky, steaming puddle of fat soaked away.

'He can't have this one!' Enoch cried. 'She's mine!'

Drusticc turned on him.

'Enoch!' she pleaded, and her voice was low and sweet.

'But I've been building her all winter. We need her for the fishing!'

'Enoch!' And now her voice was like the wind beginning to rise.

Pangur looked up at her and blinked twice. There was something strange about the hill behind her. Above the monastery the skyline had begun to prickle, like the first shoots of wheat coming through the soil.

'You said I could make her for the fishing. You promised!'

'*Enoch!*' There is no time to argue!'

The skyline was a springing forest behind her. Tall spikes, catching the light, where before there had been only rolling heather. The hair on Pangur's neck started to rise.

'Let him build his own boat if he wants to put to sea. Months, this has taken me.'

'Niall does not even have until tomorrow,' said Drusticc softly.

And she turned her face as the first whinny of horses came clearly down the slopes above her and a great shout

13

roared to the sky. The whole ridge was lined with horsemen. Light flashed on moving spears, on rolling chariots, on bright, painted shields. Like a bursting volcano they swept over the crest and came pouring down on the convent. Niall sprang to his feet. Enoch pressed back against his greasy boat.

'*Now* will you believe me?' cried Drusticc, hurling the sack of food on board and the cask after it. 'Had you forgotten that Martin was a prince? The son of Kernac, king of the Summer Isle. Own blood to warrior princes and princesses. Could you not guess what would happen? Did you imagine they would let his death go unavenged? Now! *Go!*'

The beach was quaking under their feet with the oncoming hooves. The bright spring grass vanished under a thundercloud of horses. And still they came pouring over the ridge by the thousand.

Niall took one terrified look and leapt into the boat. Enoch clung on for a desperate moment. But when he threw a glance over his shoulder, he screamed, hitched up his skirts and ran.

Drusticc heaved the boat out to sea with all her strength.

'Yee-ow!' shrieked Pangur, as its protecting shadow shot away from him. He was alone and undefended on the beach. The horses' hooves were coming at him, sharp as plough-shares, cutting everything in their path. In a streak of white, flung spray in a gale, Pangur flew through the air and wrapped his four legs around the mast of Niall's boat. He clung with his claws buried in the soft new wood.

Only Drusticc stood still, straight and tall as an ash tree, facing the army. The storm of horsemen swept down on to the beach around her, a wild ocean surging over a spray-washed rock. She disappeared. Then, screwing his head round, Pangur saw her white arm pointing at the boat. The leading horsemen wheeled, urging their ponies into the shallow water. The first spear came whistling over the stern.

'Oh, my God!' groaned Niall. 'Where are the oars?'

Above the tumult of shouting, Drusticc's clear voice

floated on the wind. 'There are no oars. Trust yourselves to the wind of God!'

Another spear grazed the side of the boat.

'Hoist the sail!' spat Pangur furiously.

'No oars! I can't! How?' The painter's hands trembled in panic among the coiled ropes.

Pangur sprang down and seized the free end in his teeth.

'Here! Pull!' he hissed.

Slowly the sail began to climb the mast. The horses were stamping through the surf in a flurry of foam. Up to their knees, their chests, their riders shouting to them, kicking them on, brandishing spears and swords through the spray.

'Faster!' moaned Pangur. 'Faster!'

The sail flapped and filled. The shining water lengthened between the boat and the avenging army. The horses were slowing now, not liking the waves that were breaking into their faces.

'Go on! Go on!' cried Pangur. 'You're sailing her! We're winning!'

He spoke too soon. Like a stone from a sling, a piebald pony shot out into the sea, braving the waves, swimming strongly. The rider was small, crouched high on its withers, heels kicking its flanks through the water, compelling the animal out into the ocean. White teeth gripped a long unsheathed sword.

A rain of arrows, faster than the wind, pelted the sea around them. The shore dwindled too slowly. The gap was closing. The white blaze of the pony's head flashed in the wake. Its eyes bulged with effort. Its nostrils were snorting water. The rider kicked it furiously.

'On, Melisant! On!' a young voice cried.

And the wind freshened. The boat scudded over the waves. Still the pony struggled to obey its rider. But it was out of its depth. The breakers were dashing into its face. The sea-bed had sunk out of reach of its hooves. Its head sank lower.

'On, Melisant! On!'

The pony was faltering with exhaustion. The ocean widened round it.

'We've done it!' yelled Niall. 'They'll never catch us now!'

With a cry of rage, the rider slid down over the floating mane. Arms flailed the sea.

'Keep away,' growled Niall. 'What's happened to the wind?'

The sail flapped ominously. The breeze fell to a whisper.

'Keep away, I tell you! Don't come any closer!'

The brown head was thrusting nearer.

'Don't you dare!' shouted Niall. 'I'm warning you!'

A small hand gripped the gunwale. Niall grabbed the water cask.

'Get off! For the last time, get back!'

A second hand grasped the side. Niall swung the cask above his head.

'Miaow!' wailed Pangur, as the horrible memory of the stool blackened his soul.

And Niall remembered. The cask wavered in his hands.

A dripping head appeared out of the waves. Bright drops fell from the sharpened edge of a sword between clenched teeth. There was a wild lurch. The curragh spun crazily as a slight figure in a splendid chequered cloak vaulted aboard. They all tumbled off balance. But when the boat steadied, the newcomer held poised aloft the long gleaming sword.

'At last I have you!' cried a young, clear voice. 'Look your last on the sun, slayer of princes. Sing your last prayers, you murdering monk! Behold! Cruimthan the avenger is in the hands of Finnglas, daughter of Kernac of the Summer Isle—and Martin's sister!'

Her sword flashed high above her head. The sun caught all
the smith's art twining along its blade. Niall threw up his
hands to shield himself. At that moment the wind sprang into
the sails again, as though it had only been waiting for
Finnglas to come. The boat leapt forward like an unleashed
hound. Finnglas tumbled one way and Niall the other.
Cruimthan clattered into the bottom of the boat. They both
grabbed for it, but Finnglas was quicker.

'It wasn't me!' gabbled Niall. 'I didn't want to kill him.
Didn't I love him like a son? It was that devil of a cat. It was
Pangur Bán. He made me do it. He made me angry. The
blow was meant for him.'

'It wasn't me,' mewed Pangur. 'You struck the blow.
Drusticc said it was you.'

Finnglas picked up the sword and rose to her feet.

'Then I must kill you both,' she said quietly.

Pangur took one terrified look at her set face and
scrambled into the bows of the boat, as far away from both of
them as he could get. When the spray wet his fur he turned.

Then, 'Look!' he mewed.

And Finnglas, twisting round, saw what he had seen.

The wind was driving the boat hard out to sea, leaving a
long, bubbling wake behind them. Far down its path,
Finnglas's pony was still struggling after them. Its nose
barely showed above the waves now. Water weighted its
sodden black and white coat. The long dark mane dragged
downwards like dank seaweed. The ears sank lower.

'Melisant!' shrieked Finnglas. 'I forgot her!'

She watched in horror as the heavy, white-blazed head
strained for air too high above it. Time and again the snorting
nostrils rose above the surface, bubbling out water only to

17

gasp more in. The eyes rolled white with fear.

'*Melisant*, wait! I'm coming!'

And she dived back into the water.

Niall let go of the sheets. The sail flapped loose, and the speed of the boat slackened suddenly.

'Are you mad?' cried Pangur. 'Sail on, while we've got the chance!'

But Niall's hands hovered on the knot that held the crossyard.

'Don't be a fool! She wants to kill us both!'

Niall looked over his shoulder at the distant shore. Thousands of warriors still blackened the beach, like a heath after fire. A single white speck showed at the water's edge.

'Drusticc is watching me.'

With a sudden rush Niall unloosed the sail and brought it tumbling down as Pangur leapt out of the way. He tried to paddle backwards with his hands, but the wind still held them off the shore.

'The oars!' he groaned. 'Why didn't she let us have oars?'

Finnglas was struggling and coughing her way back to the drowning pony. She grabbed the trailing bridle. With the last of her strength she began to fight her way back to the boat, dragging her waterlogged burden. For all the flailing of her arms she hardly seemed to move. Niall and Pangur watched helplessly as the two heads sank lower and lower in the waves. First the pony's nose disappeared from sight, then the ears. Finnglas looked round and saw only a smooth black circle in the water where it had been.

They heard her scream. Then she too vanished.

Niall and Pangur looked at each other.

'It's no good looking at me,' wailed Pangur. 'I can't swim.'

'It's so long since I did, I've forgotten how,' said Niall. 'But she's Martin's sister. I can't let her die. Not with Drusticc watching.'

He peeled off his robe. There was a mighty splash as he went overboard.

His arms threshed the water wildly; his feet drummed

against the waves. Then his stroke steadied. He turned his head sideways. 'It's all right. I'm swimming!' he gasped. Then the water rushed into his lungs and he sank.

Finnglas came up fighting for the sky. In her hand she still clutched the bridle. The huge wet weight of Melisant was threshing against her thigh underwater.

'Help!' she screamed. 'Oh, help me, somebody!'

There was a coughing behind her. A pair of great brown hands closed over hers. They heaved together.

'Pull!' gasped Niall.

But all they could feel was the weight of flesh and bone and sodden hair that was the pony, dragging at their muscles, sinking beneath them, pulling them down.

It was cold and dark under the surface. A bottomless depth, and still Finnglas was falling. Pain tearing at her lungs. Then, without warning, the great cloud-shape of Melisant was floating beside her in the murk, bubbling towards the surface. Finnglas broke the wave-tops, spluttering and triumphant.

'I've got her! I've got her! she yelled. 'You! Help me!'

But already, Melisant was sinking for the third time. Niall's hands were slipping past hers on the leather.

'We've got to let go!' he panted. 'She's too heavy for us. She'll drown us both.'

'I won't let go! I won't!' gasped Finnglas, clutching at the reins as they slithered through her fingers. 'Oh, Melis . . .'

Her cry ended in a gurgle as water filled her nose. This time she was rushing downwards with frightening speed, no breath in her lungs, no strength in her muscles. Darkness filled her eyes. She was pulling, hauling, uselessly. Then there were strong arms around her, wrestling her to the surface. She fought against them. They surfaced, with Niall gripping her wrists.

'It's too late,' he shouted. 'You can't save her. She's gone, I tell you.'

'She isn't! She isn't!' And Finnglas prepared to dive again.

'What's that in your hands?'

'Melisant!' sobbed Finnglas.

19

She looked down. Short thongs of leather were clenched uselessly in her fists. Their snapped ends floated in the water beside her. Under the weight, the sodden slender reins had broken. A cloud of bubbles rose from under the sea.

'Melisant!' she shrieked.

She watched the bubbles round her spreading. Bursting. Dying. And then the sea lay smooth as steel.

'*Melisant!*' she sobbed. 'Oh, Melisant!'

Niall dragged Finnglas with him back to the boat. It was a greasy, unstable thing to climb aboard. Pangur's back arched and he growled as Finnglas tumbled in. She collapsed in the bottom of the boat, beating her small fists against the leather.

'Melisant! Oh, Melisant! Why did you do it? Why did you come after me like that? Why were you so true, so brave?'

It's too much,' muttered Niall. 'To lose a brother and a pony in two days.'

Finnglas seized her sword. Her eyes flashed fury.

'It's all your fault! You killed Martin. I *had* to come after you. You made me do it! She was the bravest pony in the world. You made me leave her. You made me forget her!'

She got to her feet and swung the long, bright blade above her head.

'I'll kill you both now. For Martin and for Melisant, I'll kill you both.'

An arrow sang past her shoulder and buried itself in the leather side of the boat. Finnglas whirled round, shouting angrily.

'Who did that? How dare they? What vile slave fires at Finnglas, daughter of Kernac? My father will cut off the head of that man. He will hang it by the hair from his chariot-pole, and dry it over the hearth fire of Rath Daran, and hoist it on a spear over the roof-tree . . . '

'Pleasant little thing, isn't she?' said Pangur, scrambling away into the bows.

Niall grabbed the arrow and pulled it out.

'It's not you they're firing at, you silly girl, it's me. They think you're dead. They saw Melisant drown.'

Finnglas stood up and waved her sword. The boat

21

rocked wildly. Pangur tumbled off the bows and fell with a splash into the bottom of the boat.

'Yee-ow!' he shrieked, leaping up again. 'The arrow! Niall, you fool, you pulled the arrow out! Now the sea is coming in to drown us all!'

Water was bubbling silkily through the slit the arrow had left in the leather skin. Not fast. But like a well-fed baby, leaking milk between sleeping lips. Slowly the greasy water was gathering in the bottom of the boat in an ever-widening pool.

Finnglas dropped her sword and rammed the arrow back home. With a grimace of disgust Pangur Bán scooped a pawful of grease from the newly-larded gunwale and pressed it around the slit. They held their breath.

A tiny, tiny drop swelled beside the cut. The three of them watched it grow into a drip and hang, and break, rolling down into the greasy pool. A second drop followed. There were no more.

'Quick!' hissed Pangur to Niall. 'Get her sword! Now!'

But Finnglas's hand shot out before his.

'Don't you dare! I'll kill the first one who moves!'

Niall rocked on his feet, measuring the distance between them. Then his shoulders dropped.

'It's no good. I'm a painter, not a Cornish wrestler. One false move and she'd gut me like a pilchard.'

Another flight of arrows spattered the sea around them.

'All right! All right!' roared Niall. 'Can't you see I'm going?'

Under his hands the big dark leather sail climbed to the top of the mast. The wind caught it. Niall grabbed the trailing sheet and hauled it in. The wind filled the belly of the sail. The boat leapt forward.

'Where are you taking me?' shouted Finnglas, thrown back on the thwart. 'Turn the boat round!'

'Are you mad?' said Niall. 'Your father's men would spit us like larks on a skewer.'

He looked round. Kernac's army still milled in the shallow water on the edge of the beach. Kernac's chariot glittered in the sun. Kernac's horses pawed the water. And

Drusticc still stood watching.

'Take me back to my father,' ordered Finnglas, levelling Cruimthan at Niall's chest.

He licked his lips. 'Be reasonable,' he said. 'You know I can't.' He watched the quivering blade uneasily.

Finnglas rose to her feet and raised the sword. Niall's hand moved unsteadily on the steering oar. The boat began to swing across the wind. The shore revolved to meet it, till it lay broadside across the waves, and faltered. The square sail flapped, fell slack, and billowed back against the mast. Gently the boat drifted backwards, out to sea.

'For the last time,' said Finnglas, grasping her sword above her head. 'Take me back to my father.'

Niall looked at her helplessly. 'I can't,' he said. 'This boat won't sail against the wind.'

There was a long silence. Pangur let out a wail of desolation. They looked at Finnglas. Her eyes were huge in her salt-white face. Cruimthan dropped.

Watching her closely, Niall moved the steering oar round. At once the wind bellied the sail in front of the mast. The boat kicked up its heels and took off at a gallop. High on the bows, Pangur stood with his tail blown back and his ears flat against his head. The sky grew dark. Foam flew between the sea and the lowering clouds. Kernac the king had vanished behind ramparts of grey water. Drusticc had gone.

As the light grew less, the noise became greater. The cracking of ropes, the creak of untried wood, the crash of waves and the rushing, singing swoop of Enoch's new curragh flying east before the growing storm.

5

The sky was as wet as the ocean. Pangur Bán's fur squelched as he clung to the halyards. The gale whipped the warmth from his skinny body and flung it away over the cold sea. He was the ghost of a white cat on a dark ship.

'Haul it down! Haul it down!' he miaowed to Niall, as the heavy leather sail cracked like a whip and the ropes sprang taut as chariot poles.

But Niall was suddenly enjoying himself. His big hands eased the sail, giving with the hardest gusts, letting it fill and swell as the wind steadied again.

'Not bad for a landlubber! I'm getting the hang of it,' he roared above the creaks and crashings.

'How much did Enoch know about boat-building?' moaned Pangur.

He picked his way angrily through the sloshing sea-water in the bottom of the boat to where the arrow stood up out of the pierced leather. As the boat twisted over the broaching waves, the water was trickling slowly in from the cut.

'We ought to bail, but we haven't even a cup! How long is it till morning?'

'What does it matter?' bellowed Niall. 'A man may drown as easily in the sunshine as in the dark.'

'It's all right for you. You can swim.'

'So could the pony. It didn't save her. The sea's too big for any of us now.'

'Ssh! Keep your voice down!'

They both looked forward. Finnglas sat hunched in the bows, nursing her unblooded sword on her knees, like a mother with her child. As a burst of spray broke over the bows they glimpsed her face white in the gloom. Rain plastered her dark hair to her head and ran in rivers down the neck of her cloak. She did not flinch from the waves. She did not shiver as the spray drenched her chest.

'Maybe you're right,' muttered Niall. 'Perhaps I should run down the sail.'

'Yes! Yes!'

Niall's fingers fumbled for the knots in the dark. The crossyard slid into the bottom of the boat in a crumpled heap of leather and cord.

Finnglas turned silently.

'The wind's too strong!' Niall yelled to her. 'We'll have to ride out the storm.'

The boat slowed and floundered. The gale raced past them, on into the east. Around them the noise of the breaking sea grew louder. They could feel the waves pushing against the boat, turning it, rolling it.

'I don't like this!' Niall said uneasily. 'Maybe we were safer running before it.'

He hauled on the steering oar. Slowly he forced the bows of the boat back into the set of the wind and they were riding with the sea once more. Great swooping rollers overtook them, tossing them to the sky, dropping them like a stone. In spite of the tumult around them, it seemed strangely silent. The boat no longer sang.

'I'm not enjoying this,' Niall repeated. 'I don't feel as if we're in control any more.'

'Listen!' said Pangur.

'I can't hear anything.'

'Ssh!'

'It's someone singing.' Finnglas's clear voice came unexpectedly out of the darkness.

Niall was clambering to his feet.

'Yes! ... It's *women* singing!'

'It must be the wind in the rigging,' Pangur said quickly.

'No! Can't you hear them? There are voices. Words.'

He was starting towards the mast, leaving the tiller abandoned.

The soaked hair on Pangur's neck began to rise. His claws crept out of their velvet sheath. A low growl thrilled in his throat. He could hear the voices now, hear the words singing in an unknown language, binding, compelling words. Calling them, drawing them, summoning them. His back arched in fear and his claws dug into the yielding wood.

'The sail!' cried Niall. 'We must follow them!'

In panting haste he fumbled for the ropes.

'*No!*' Pangur sprang at him. His claws buried themselves in Niall's hands.

With a roar Niall threw him off. He made for the tiller. 'We're going the wrong way! We have to turn north!'

Finnglas leapt past him and reached the tiller first. One hand held it steady; the other levelled her sword at him.

'Get back! One more step and I'll stick you like a hog.'

Pangur stood between them, back arched, and spitting. Niall stumbled back. With a cry of relief Pangur rubbed against Finnglas's legs. She kicked him aside, still watching Niall.

The singing was rising all about them now, sweeter than honey, clearer than bells, purer than snowflakes.

Niall rushed back to the mast. The crossyard began to rise. The wind sprang into the shuddering sail even as it rose.

'Stop him! Stop him!'

Pangur streaked across the boat. He leapt for Niall's neck, claws scratching at his shoulders, fur muffling Niall's ears, trying to shut out the song. He clung like a leech, defying Niall's tearing hands.

The music rose from the sea like moonrise out of darkness. As though every star beyond the clouds was singing. As though the gale was a river of song. As though every drop of flying spray was a separate note of music soaring out of an ocean of harmony. They were sailing over a sea of song.

'Let me go! Let me go!' Niall wrestled with Pangur like a madman.

'Too late!' cried Finnglas pointing.

Niall wrenched his head round. Lights blazed in front of them out of the darkness. A swooping ship twenty times the size of theirs. Crowded with sail. Lanterns swaying from the mast. Lanterns held aloft along the sides. Men jostling each other, straining forward, the lantern light full on their eager faces. Pulled irresistably on by chains of song. The ship drove past the curragh's bows like a wild stallion across the path of a rabbit. Her sails were spread on a broad reach, going north.

'They're following the singers! They're going to find them! They'll get there first!'

Niall beat wildly at the clinging Pangur. The tide of song rose higher and higher, drowning their senses.

'Let me *go*!'

He tore Pangur's claws from his neck and sprang for the steering oar.

'Wait!'

With Finnglas's cry, the crystal music splintered. Echoes of a mighty crash ran through the darkness. The curragh shuddered as a violent wave struck it. The lights vanished. The singing stopped. Deep beneath them, like the echo of women's laughter, the last notes came bubbling up and faded away. The wind moaned wetly in the halyards. They were alone on the ocean.

'But they were *here*!' groaned Niall, beating his fists against the sides. 'The singers! I heard them! They were *here*! And I have lost them.'

6

'Dawn,' said Finnglas. 'The sky is turning green.'

The sun rose on a buttercup morning. Petals of gold flowered out of the emerald cups of the waves. A wide, wind-washed sky. And all around them, a dark skein of flotsam was spreading on the tide. It rocked gently just below the heaving waves. The sea slipped a smooth surface over it, like a shroud.

Pangur leaned over the gunwale and dipped a paw down into the sliding side of a wave.

'Wood,' he said. 'A broken plank, I think.'

He let it go. The next wave brought something softer. His unsheathed claws tangled in it, and the weight almost dragged him into the sea. Finnglas helped him haul it aboard.

'A cloak,' she said. 'Empty. As ours would have been if Niall had had his way.'

They sailed among the flotsam, while the seagulls chanted psalms over them.

'The singers,' Niall repeated helplessly. 'They followed the singers.'

'Remember you're a monk,' growled Pangur. 'You should be singing the litany for the dead.'

Then he remembered how they had buried Martin. He wished he had not spoken.

But Finnglas steered the boat on, peering intently over the side at the wreckage. Snapped timbers, trailing ropes, fragments of clothing.

'You'd be wasting your time. There's nobody here,' she said curiously. 'Not a lock of hair, not a hand, not one drowned face. They have all vanished under the sea. Where Melisant went. I should have followed her.'

Weeks later, a peak grew above the waves, blue against the white horizon. Niall steered for it.

White spray curled over rocks. They looked at each other doubtfully.

'Best lower the sail,' said Niall. 'How did she expect us to make landfall without a paddle?'

The wind washed them past the rocks. The curragh came tiptoeing into an unknown cove. They looked about them in silence. A black line of seaweed, white sand, wind rustling the grass on the dunes.

'Well,' said Niall heartily. 'At least, there'll be water. We can fill the cask. We've been a month at sea.'

Pangur ran his triangular tongue over dry gums. He leapt from the bows on to the beach and quickly drew back his paws from the hot sand. Finnglas followed, holding Cruimthan clear of the water. Niall waded after. They stood on the lonely beach, swaying on the steady ground, suspicious of each other, tired.

'There's bound to be water,' Niall said again. 'There must be a stream somewhere.'

Pangur found it, winding under elder bushes. When he had drunk, he mewed loudly with hunger.

'I suppose you expect me to catch fish for you,' grumbled Niall. 'Without a line and hooks. We haven't even a bent pin between us.'

They both turned and looked hard at Finnglas. Her chequered cloak was fastened with a circle of twisted red gold, set with a cross of garnets.

She glared at them. 'Take it! You have robbed me of a brother and a horse. What do I care if you steal my gold as well!'

She threw the brooch down on to the sand in front of them. The cloak slipped down behind her, and she stood in her warrior's tunic and breeches with the royal collar of gold about her throat.

Niall picked up the jewel. It lay in his palm like drops of blood. He turned it over hastily and fashioned the pin into a hook. His strong hands delved into the sand for worms and he unravelled a long thread from the sleeve of his gown.

Then, almost happily, he set off along the rocks to sit with his bare feet dangling in the cool water.

'I'm tired,' said Finnglas crossly.

She trailed her sword into a hollow of the dunes and threw herself down beside it, hiding her face in her cloak.

Pangur moved cautiously away and began to wash. Presently he could feel his eyelids weighted with sunshine and the weakness of hunger. He looked at the sleeping Finnglas, clutching her long sword like a child with her best-loved toy. Quietly Pangur walked away through the long grass, looking back over his shoulder. At last he peered round from behind a clump of sea-holly. Finnglas was no longer in sight. With a sigh of relief, Pangur curled himself into the tiniest ball possible in a shaded cup of soft sand, and closed his eyes.

He woke to the smell of grilling mackerel. Niall had lit a fire on the beach. The juice bubbled from the fish as the skins blistered and cracked. Without waiting to be asked, Pangur seized his share. He burnt his tongue, but at last he was full and happy. Finnglas still slept. One fish lay warm and crisp on a stone by the fire.

'We'd better save it for her,' said Niall.

'Why?' asked Pangur. But they both knew.

Night fell, and the moon rose on a tide of silver. Finnglas had eaten and sat hunched by the fire. Pangur crouched in the shadows. But Niall paced at the water's edge.

Suddenly they heard him shout in excitement.

'Look! Look here! Pangur!'

Pangur went racing down over the damp sand. Under the moon a pale foam curled and creamed among the bladder-wrack. The waves were tossing fragments of jetsam up and sucking them back again. One by one they let go of their burdens and left them on the newly-wet sand as the tide fell. Here a spar, there a thwart, beyond, a split length of plank, an empty boot.

Pangur drew back in fear. 'It's the same as before! Another ship gone down.'

'That's what I mean!' shouted Niall. 'Don't you see?'

30

'Yes. The singers have led a boatload of souls to their death.'

'Not *death*, Pangur! Finnglas was right! *Where are their bodies?*'

Pangur looked quickly round the bay. Wind and tide had herded the wreckage here. What had not yet come to rest bobbed on the waves. He scanned it keenly. There was nothing that resembled the pale face or hands of a man.

Niall cried out, 'Don't you understand, Pangur? They're not dead! They have followed the singers. They have found them under the sea. They are with them now!'

His eyes began to sparkle in the moonlight. He was staring at the curragh.

'No!' cried Pangur. 'You can't! Niall, don't even think of it!'

'They have found them. They have found those singers! And I've been left behind!'

'Niall? Pangur? What's the matter?' Finnglas's clear voice came echoing over the shore. She stood in the moonlight, between Niall and the boat. The drawn blade of Cruimthan glinted silver in her hand.

Seeing her, the monk fell silent. He let Pangur lead him up the beach and lay down under the trees beyond the dunes.

But the white cat set himself to watch Niall through the long hours of the night.

7

He should have warned Finnglas. They could have shared the watch between them. But Pangur was afraid of her sharp sword and her glaring eyes and her hard boots that kicked him out of the way. So he kept his distance from her and settled himself on the branch of a tree above Niall. As the slow hours crept on, he crouched in the darkness, his ears pricked and his green eyes wide and staring. He did not move.

But he must have slept. It was Finnglas who woke him with a great shout. Pangur nearly fell out of the tree with fright. Her voice came sharp and angry over the dunes.

'Niall! Pangur Bán! Where are you hiding? I know you're there. Come out at once!'

Pangur Bán peered down from his branch. He could see nothing. No stars, not a glimmer of moonlight. A damp, dark fog stole between the trees. His hair began to bristle with fear. She was hunting him with her sword to kill him in the dark.

Finnglas's voice was closer now. Higher.

'Pangur? Are you there, Pangur Bán?'

He lay still on the branch, trying to quiet his trembling.

'Pangur? Don't say you've left me, too? Oh, *please*, Pangur!'

His eyes widened. That sounded more frightened than frightening. Pangur sprang silently on to the soft wet grass and stalked towards her warily.

The toe of a boot caught him suddenly in the ribs and sent him sprawling.

'*Mia-ow!*'

She dived after him.

'Pangur! It *is* you! Oh, Pangur!'

Hands closed round his writhing body. He fought to get free.

'Where's Niall, Pangur? I can't find him. I couldn't find either of you!'

'Of course you couldn't, you silly fool. I was up a tree, wasn't I? Do you think I'd sleep within reach of your murdering sword?'

She was angry then.

'*Murdering?* You dare say that to *me*? You who murdered Martin?'

'Grrr!' He spat at her as the pain of the memory hit back at him. 'What do you want, if not to kill us in our sleep?'

'I woke up and heard singing. I came looking for you. But ...'

'Singing!' He went suddenly still in her hands.

'Listen.'

He heard it then. Welling up from the deep, ringing round the sky, rolling in towards them round the rocks.

'Oh, no!'

With a twisting leap he was out of her grasp and running to the hollow where he had left Niall sleeping. The flattened grass still smelt of his warm brown robe.

'He's gone! ... The curragh!'

They raced for the shore, springing paws and running leather boots, over the dunes, ploughing the glimmering sand. Too late. The singing soared into the mist, and stopped. There were only the waves grating on the pebbles. The beach was empty.

'Oh, no! Not Niall too!'

'The boat! Where has it gone? Pangur, what has he done?'

'Can't you see? He has followed the voices. He has put out to sea on the tide. It's your fault! You told him there were no bodies, and he believed you. He thinks they are alive, following the song, finding the singers at last, somewhere under the sea. Now Niall has followed them too.'

'Then he's taken our boat? He's gone to his death and left me marooned on this island? How *could* he? Hasn't he done enough to me already? How will I ever get home now?'

'*Miaow!* What about me?'

She rounded on him. 'You stupid cat! Why didn't you tell me? I wouldn't have let him! I'd have watched in the curragh with Cruimthan in my hand. I'd have run him through the entrails before I let him take it. You *fool*, Pangur!'

He backed away, growling.

'Fool, is it? Do you think we'd have trusted you? Do you think we'd have let you sleep in the boat? How do we know you wouldn't have sailed away yourself and left us here to die? Didn't you threaten to kill us?'

'And why shouldn't I? Wasn't it justice? Didn't you kill Martin and Melisant?'

'*We* killed Melisant? That was you! *You* rode her into the sea. *You* left her to drown!'

'I didn't! I didn't! Oh, I didn't *mean* to leave her!'

'Oh, none of us *mean* to. I didn't *mean* to spoil Niall's Gospel. Niall didn't *mean* to kill Martin. You didn't *mean* to drown Melisant. But they're dead, aren't they? And now we've lost Niall too.'

'Why should you care? He tried to kill you too, didn't he?'

'I made him angry,' Pangur murmured miserably. 'And he's all I've got left now . . . after Martin.'

Finnglas began to stride out over the rocks. Pangur heard the slap of her boots going away in the mist. He was all alone. Presently he began to follow her, picking his paws carefully over the slimy seaweed. The warm, human smell of her came to him out of the darkness. She was not Martin, but he had no one else.

They came to the end of the rocks, where small waves plopped against the stone. Finnglas stood staring down at the water.

'Pangur? What if he's right? What if those sailors didn't drown? What if there's a kingdom under the sea where the singing comes from? Pangur . . .!'

'No! Finnglas, come away!'

'Can't you see? *Melisant!* We never saw her body either! She didn't drown! I know she didn't. She's down there.

Under the waves. Still galloping. Alive! Pangur, I'm going to find her!'

'No, Finnglas! You can't do it! You'll be drowned.'

'I can! I must! I will die, or find her!'

'You mustn't go! You can't leave me alone!'

He leapt on to her shoulder and clung with his claws.

'Get off, or I'll be taking you with me. I'm going now!'

'No! I can't swim!'

'I'm going to sink, not swim. If she is anywhere alive, she's at the bottom of the sea.'

He felt her jump. There was a tremendous splash, and then a roaring in his ears. The sound of darkness. Weight clouding his eyeballs. His throat gasped for air. He opened his mouth and breathed in a torrent of water.

8

Pangur choked and spat out water. His lungs opened again and water rushed in. He coughed it back. Out. And in. Out, and in. And then he realized. He was breathing water, like drowning in wind.

When his throbbing brain had accepted this truth, he opened his eyes. Cold darkness. It was silly of him to have expected it to be light under the sea when it was night above. His claws were still buried in Finnglas's shoulder.

'Finnglas?'

'Let go. You're hurting me.'

Their voices bubbled strangely towards each other. He eased his grip from her flesh, but still he grasped her cloak securely. He did not want to be alone in an ocean that seemed vaster than ever before.

'It's worse than the fog on land,' he said softly, for he did not know what might be listening. 'There's up and down to get lost in, as well as forwards and backwards.'

'Go back if you're afraid,' whispered Finnglas.

Pangur peeped over his shoulder into the unfathomable wetness through which they had dived.

'I don't think I know where "back" *is*.'

Finnglas was swimming away from him, towing him on the end of her streaming cloak. He scrabbled with his paws to keep up with her.

She checked suddenly.

Out of the gloom flowered two round yellow eyes. Then another pair. And another, and another. Like a field of dandelions, all in twos. With a swift kick Finnglas shot upwards. All the yellow eyes rolled up to watch her through the darkness.

They swam on.

A trail of light shimmered towards them. Silver phosphorescence, shining, twining, writhing, hunting. This time they dived. Two water snakes coiled slowly over their heads, looking downwards.

They crept along the bottom now, close together, feeling the brush of sand and the scrape of rocks. Waiting for something else, unseen.

'Are you sure it's safe?' moaned Pangur.

'Safe? I didn't come here to be safe.'

But her hand brushed along his side and closed round his paw. He felt a little better.

'Where are we going?'

She had no time to answer. Another light was rushing towards them, faster than before. Small as a candle-flame in the distance one instant, but all at once growing, twisting, spreading, leaping. Pangur struggled to back away. A great mist of golden hair shot past his eyes. As he shrank back, a fish-tail whipped around them, slender, supple, scales blue as ice but flickering like fire. Pangur felt himself drop into cold space as Finnglas let go of his paw and reached for her sword.

But it had gone, with a final flourish of a forked fan-tail that was as green as emeralds. They saw it die to a pale-blue pinprick, like the evening star. Then, as they watched, it began to circle them, at the same distance, like a charioteer with an unbroken colt on the end of a rope.

Suddenly it came rushing back, fast as the wind, all blue and gold, rippling, dancing in front of their eyes. Finnglas raised her sword.

'Who are *you*, that come without the singing?'

The voice was high, ringing, chiming like bells. It spoke to Pangur of the convent on the cliffs, the nuns walking to vespers at the end of the day. But it ended in laughter, like the whinny of a pony. Finnglas caught her breath.

'Take us to the others,' she said, steadying her voice. 'Take us where you take all those who come to the kingdom under the sea.'

'*King*dom, is it?' And the sea shook with her mockery. 'The mermaids own no *king* in Ancofva, the Halls of Forgetting.'

A blue-white arm reached out slowly and touched Finnglas's face.

'You sound young, boy,' the mermaid said wonderingly. 'The voice not broken. And you came without even waiting for the singing.' Then she threw back her golden hair and laughed like a waterfall. 'Follow Morwenna, then!'

She shot away from them in a cloud of phosphorescent bubbles. Finnglas leapt after her, still gripping her sword, with Pangur struggling in her wake.

'Are you mad?' he panted. 'She's a mermaid! You're not going to trust her?'

'I trust none but Cruimthan,' said Finnglas grimly. 'But it was for this that I came.'

'Is she taking us to Niall?' asked Pangur after a while.

'It is not Niall I am looking for. It's Melisant.'

The fish-tail flicked round and came swooping back towards them. A halo of hair parted to show a face like a snowdrop, white, green-eyed, smiling sweetly.

'Come! Follow!' Her laughter was like the tinkling of icicles. She darted away.

They stretched out their legs and found themselves loping along with effortless strides. There was water under their feet, water against their chests, water flowing past their ears and tangling in bubbles in their hair. Now they raced down long warm currents, with sudden shocks of cold coming at them from unseen eddies. The ice-blue shimmer led them through the dark, like a will-o'-the-wisp.

The darkness began to thin into a grey twilight. Pangur could see Finnglas's hand around the hilt of Cruimthan. The blade gleamed cold and slippery as the mermaid's tail. Pangur dropped further behind her.

The mermaid came racing back to them, hair streaming behind her, like a sheepdog puppy, herding ducklings.

'Hurry! It's almost morning.'

Shoals of tiny grey fish trooped past them. Rays lifted huge plate-like bodies from the sea-bed and dropped invisible again into the sand. Dark unnamed shadows drifted overhead and were swallowed up in the caverns of the rocks.

Without warning, there was a flash of the forked tail in

front of them, and the mermaid dived into a cleft of coral-crusted rocks. Pangur and Finnglas looked at each other uncertainly. Then they forced themselves downwards, following her.

The crevice in the sea-bed was cold and still, shadowed from the coming dawn. Only a curtain of sea-lettuce shivered inside a hollow arch of rock. A white hand parted the curtain and beckoned to them.

Holding Cruimthan in both hands in front of her, Finnglas stepped through the arch, with Pangur creeping at her heels.

Light cascaded on to a circle of silver sand. Spirals of shells shimmered with mother-of-pearl. Periwinkles studded the walls. The rock climbed above their heads, vertical, cylindrical, reaching far up to the swaying surface of the sea and a pale circle of sky. And as they lifted their heads, dawn broke. They saw the whole depth of water turn translucent and flower into opalescent rose and turquoise, shot through with sparks of gold. Across this jewelled eye of the ocean the shoals of grey fish turned to coral striped with black, pink spots on peacock blue, scarlet with silver.

'Welcome.'

They blinked and looked down. The mermaid was lying on a couch made soft with fringed seaweed. Curtains of fishnets looped above her, hung from the rusted points of old spears and harpoons. Out of these spoils she smiled at them without human warmth.

'So! Who dares come under the sea uninvited, and follows Morwenna to her chamber?'

With a quick twitch of her tail she swam around Finnglas, touching her bound hair, stroking her cheek, feeling her clothes.

'So young,' she said again. 'And yet so fine. With the royal gold about his throat. A pretty boy, with a sword almost as big as himself. A pretty, rosy, royal boy, wearing a prince's cloak.'

She turned swiftly to Pangur.

'And what are *you*, pray? I have never seen your like beneath the sea.'

'I'm a cat.'

'A cat? What is a cat? Are you good to eat?'

'Cats eat fish. Not the other way round,' Pangur said sharply. 'And you didn't catch us. We came of our own free will. I expect I'm very bad to eat. I'm a monastery cat. I came here looking for a monk. Have you got him?'

She threw back her head. Bubbles of laughter came pouring out of her throat. She twisted her tail in delight.

'A monk! Yes, I caught a monk! Think of it, a monk following the mermaids! A monk down *here*, in the Halls of Forgetting!'

And the rocks pealed with the echoes of her laughter.

'I have snared men. Oh, hundreds, thousands of men. Dogs, sometimes. Even a cargo of horses. But you, you ... cat. I think you will make only a mouthful for the Pengoggen.' Her green eyes glared into Pangur's.

Finnglas caught her arm and whirled her round.

'Horses! Did you say you had horses?'

The mermaid turned her face in a sunburst of yellow hair. The fierce light softened in her eyes as she stared at Finnglas. She sidled closer and curved her tail around the other's legs, laying her golden head on Finnglas's shoulder, stroking Finnglas's arm. Finnglas flinched. The mermaid's voice was sweet as liquid birdsong.

'But you, my pretty boy. Do not be afraid. The Pengoggen shall not have you for his feasting. It was well that I found you when I did. And well for me that I was alone when I found you. Look how soft its cheek is, and how hairless. How fine the clothes. How delicate its flesh. It is a thousand years since we sang down such a princeling to Ancofva. Even the Sea Witch would grow young again to look at him. So young. So fair. And mine. All mine. How long can I keep you here in my chamber? How long before the Sea Witch smells you?'

She took Finnglas's hand in her cold white fingers and started to draw her to the bed. Finnglas struggled against her.

'No! The horses! Tell me about the horses!'

'Forget the horses. Forget the past. Forget the Earth. Come. Come to Morwenna. And I shall sing you songs the

40

like of which no Earthman ever heard. Songs that it would break your heart to hear and not to follow.'

And she opened pale lips in her skull-white face and began to sing. Like bells over Christmas snow, like a spring from the mountain, like larks at sunrise, and all the time she sang she was swimming round Finnglas stirring the glittering sand so that her tail shimmered like a mist of forget-me-nots.

'Stop it!' cried Finnglas. 'I don't want to hear your singing. The *horses*! Where are the horses?'

The song broke off. The forget-me-not tail quivered and lay still in the water. The voice hardened into ice.

'You close your ears against my singing? The song that all Earthmen sell their souls to hear? For each day of such song they give a year of their lives on Earth. *You*! What *are* you then? Who has dared to come into the chamber of Morwenna?'

The white hands rose in front of her, the nails hooked like talons. Finnglas's hands flew to her scabbard.

'I am Finnglas, daughter of Kernac, princess of the Summer Isle. And I come seeking my brave horse, Melisant.'

The great tail cracked like a threshing flail.

'A *girl*! An Earthmaid! . . . An *Earthmaid*! *Here*!'

Morwenna crouched before Finnglas, eyes flashing like drawn steel. Her soft white arms ended in finger-nails pointed as lobsters' claws. But there was fear in her face. Finnglas's hands seized Cruimthan. The long blade glittered in the dawn.

They faced each other. Cruimthan pointed steadily at Morwenna's breast. Morwenna's hands were outspread, like a wrestler's, waiting to spring.

'For the last time!' cried Finnglas. 'Where are the horses?'

And she lunged for Morwenna's heart. But the mermaid's tail was quicker. With a great lash of her night-blue fins she struck Finnglas behind the knees and sent her sprawling forward. The sword skidded across the sand.

'Finnglas!' squeaked Pangur, backing towards the door.

But the girl was quickly on her feet again, grabbing the sword, as Morwenna circled her now like a hungry shark.

'Woman! Earthmaid!' she stormed. Her voice clashed against the rocks like the clatter of weapons in an armoury. 'How dare you come here? It is *men* we sing for, *men* who follow us, *men* we draw down with spells and bind to us for ever under the sea. How dare you follow! Woman! Earthmaid! It is death to enter the palace of the mermaids, to speak to them of Earth and break our spell!'

Swift as a swordfish, she swooped on Finnglas from behind. Finnglas struggled to turn the sword on her. White arms locked around brown, twisting, straining, fighting. Like a bee and a wasp, they closed in mortal combat. Their whirling anger sent the sand buzzing in spirals, flying upwards like a tornado. A hail of tiny shells spun outwards, stinging, bruising, striking against the rocks. Pangur dodged

43

further back and hid behind the curtains of sea-lettuce.

Through a crack he watched the writhing blue and russet. The gleam of red-gold round Finnglas's neck. The emerald of Morwenna's tail-fin. Whirling, whirling in their panting anger. But Finnglas was tiring. Her hands struggled to lift the heavy sword again. There was shifting sand beneath her booted feet. And her arms were slipping, slipping against Morwenna's fish-scales. She stumbled to her knees as Morwenna let go of her hair.

With a trumpet cry of triumph Morwenna dived towards the bed.

'Finnglas! Look out! The spears!' yelled Pangur.

Finnglas flung herself forward with a desperate effort. She reached the bed first and stood backed against it, her sword raised for the last time above Morwenna's head.

'Now!' she cried. 'Cruimthan wins! Take me to Melisant.'

But with a great peal of laughter, Morwenna grabbed the fishnet curtains around the bed and brought them tumbling down on Finnglas's head. Finnglas screamed and lashed blindly out with her sword. With the flicker of a fin Morwenna whipped the rope around her legs and brought her crashing forward on to the sand. But still the small brown hand clutched at Cruimthan, knuckles showing white as she sought for a target. At the third twist of the rope, she cried out in pain. Morwenna lashed her arms cruelly to her body, and the sword dropped from her grasp. Morwenna's tail knocked it away. The jewelled hilt lay on the floor, bright in the morning sun, just out of reach.

Morwenna went on wrapping the mesh around Finnglas, till she was trussed and bound to a spear, like a deer that has fallen to the hunter.

Pangur took one terrified look at her twitching body and hid his white face in the shadows beyond the doorway.

'*Now!*' panted Morwenna, in a voice like bagpipes. 'Now you shall see what happens to women who would break the spell of mermaids. The Pengoggen shall have you when the full moon rises. When he has feasted, there will be nothing left of you but white, picked bones, right down to

44

your little ankles. Nothing to stir the hearts of mortal men. Nothing to make them stop their ears to our song. Nothing to lift their souls to the living sky and the Earth they have forgotten. Nothing, nothing, nothing to break the spell that makes, that keeps them ours, ours now, ours always, in Ancofva, the realms of Forgetting.'

With difficulty, she began to drag Finnglas's trussed body out of the chamber. Pangur shrank further back into the crevice. At last it floated free in the open passages of the sea-bed. Morwenna raised her hands to her lips and blew a fluting whistle.

Two great shadows came swimming towards them. Fish-tails huger than Morwenna's, blue-black in the clouded depths. Two mermen with pale, sad faces. Morwenna leaned back against the wall, panting and laughing. She flicked her tail towards Finnglas.

'For the Pengoggen,' she said. 'Another offering.'

The mermen stared down at the shrouded bundle, then turned their heads slowly to look at each other.

'Now?' they whispered.

'Yes. Now!'

She darted in front of them, swimming back the way she had led Pangur and Finnglas. Behind her, the mermen shouldered the ends of the spear, carrying the netted form of Finnglas. And beneath them crept a small white cat, keeping low under the overhanging rocks.

In the chamber they had left, the waves grew still. The flying sand began to settle. Grain by grain it drifted down until it covered the bright blade of Cruimthan. When the turquoise water cleared, the avenging sword was seen no more.

Morwenna turned sharply into a darker alley, where rocks like thunder clouds towered up from muddy depths. Black weed tossed restlessly to and fro. The water grew chill. Small fish came hurrying past, nervously, as though they could not wait to get away. Still they dropped deeper. The sea grew darker. Morwenna herself became the colour of midnight, only the crescent white of her arms glimmering like a moon through fog. The mermen were silent. Under their grim shadow Pangur sidled like a small white crab.

Abruptly the sheltering rocks ended. There was a sense of cold, black space. Morwenna backed away and motioned the mermen forward. Gently they lowered the body of Finnglas from their pale shoulders on to the mud. It lay there, writhing. A stream of bubbles rose from it. The mermen pressed back between the rocks as though eager to be gone from the place.

But Morwenna plucked from her hair three cowrie shells. Her white hand dropped one over the head of Finnglas. '*Cosoleth!*' she cried into the dark. 'Peace to you, most beautiful of sleepers!'

An ice-cold wave shuddered against Pangur's face.

Morwenna swam back hurriedly. She turned and threw another shell over Finnglas's chest. '*Lorgan!*' she called, her voice shivering. 'The moon is growing. Be merciful to us.'

The sea-bed was shaking beneath Pangur's feet.

Morwenna could hardly hold herself still. She hurled the last shell over Finnglas's legs. '*Arluth Pengoggen!*' she said in a small, trembling whisper. 'An offering from the mermaids!'

Then she turned and fled as fast as she could.

Pangur crouched, too terrified to move.

The mud heaved. The water thickened chokingly. Out of the murk two huge red eyes rose in front of him, like dawn in hell. There was a commotion in the gloom, like a moving forest, wavering, feeling, smelling, finding Finnglas. The red eyes lowered. Above the drumming in his ears, Pangur heard a hideous sucking. Helpless with horror, he watched Finnglas slither away into the murk. The red eyes dimmed and died. Even to be left alone in the darkness seemed merciful after that.

'Finnglas,' he whispered. He turned the other way. 'Niall?' he said helplessly.

No one answered.

Lost and lonely, heavy with guilt, a small white cat went creeping away from the place of death.

10

No one looked curiously at Pangur, stealing along the bottom of the sea. Herds of fishes, button bright, whisked past him. The wide clefts between the rocks were like city streets, the water cornflower blue and the surface rippling with sunshine. He was too shocked to know where he was going. His feet took him back the only way he knew, to Morwenna's chamber. But he crept past the opening with his head averted. He could not bear to see, even in memory, Finnglas, struggling, snared, bound, delivered to death. He scurried on in a hopeless daze.

The way was climbing now, a wide stairway in the rock. Sun warmed the water above him that shone pale green as birch leaves. Might there be land beyond?

But now he could hear singing. The unearthly voices that had echoed through the storm were now ringing through the sunshine, humming like bells, carolling like flutes. And like the rhythm of gongs, came the laughter of men's voices. The stairs were still climbing. Wearily he hauled himself up another step and lifted his head. A moment later he sprang back in surprise, off the highest step, and went tumbling backwards down into the rocking sea.

He hung swaying in the water and listened for a shout. But no one had noticed. Patiently, with eyes alert this time, he picked his way back to the top.

Two more mermen were guarding the stair. Huge blue-black tails, finned with silver, hung down on either side of the steps. But their heads were turned away from Pangur, watching wistfully. Beyond them, all the shallow floor of the sea was thronged with mermaids. Brighter than flowers, irridescent, tumbling with quicksilver movements in and out of the waves like leaping mackerel. And making enchanted music as they swam. And lolling in the midst of the weaving, spell-binding mermaids were hundreds of men. Human men. With beatific smiles on their faces as they listened. The scale-bright tails of the mermaids whisked past them, over them, round them. And the smiles of the men broadened as the golden hair rained on their faces, and the singing circled them with silver chains. It was the dancing-floor of Ancofva, the Place of Forgetting.

Hundreds of sea-boots, hundreds of sailors' cloaks, dozens of jewelled warriors' belts and tunics. But there, resting against a rock, one familiar brown robe.

'Niall!'

With a squawk of joy Pangur Bán fled straight to him. Under the mermaids, dodging the plough-sharp tail fins, through the seaweed, over the sailors and the chequered knees of the warriors. He sprang on to Niall's reclining chest as Morwenna soared to the surface and lay there like a wind-tossed bluebell. Pangur's claws dug into the monk's flesh.

'Niall! For the love of heaven, take that stupid grin off your face. Don't you know me? It's me, Pangur Bán!'

'Eh? What?'

Niall looked down dreamily and disengaged the cat's claws.

'What are you? I haven't seen you here before, have I?'

'Seen me? You tried to kill me once! You *must* remember me!'

A slight faraway pain crossed Niall's face. He rubbed his forehead. Pangur grabbed the neck of his robe and pulled.

'Niall! Wake up! Finnglas is in terrible danger. You remember Finnglas? The girl with the pony. Martin's sister. Remember, Niall! *Martin!*'

The smile faded from Niall's face. An unnamable sorrow squeezed a tear from his eye. But his mind was blank.

'Martin! Oh, *Niall*! You *can't* have forgotten Martin!' pleaded Pangur. 'Oh, come on, please! The Pengoggen's going to eat Finnglas. If you don't come quickly, he may have started already. You *must* save her. Remember! Remember Martin!'

Like winter lightning, Morwenna shot downwards.

48

'Vermin!' she shrieked. 'You again! What are you saying to him?'

Her nails speared the water, aiming for Pangur's eyes. He sprang away.

'After the creature! Don't let him escape! He is the spy of Earthwomen. He could spoil everything!'

A ring of mermaids, clear-eyed and hunting, came racing in.

'EARTHWOMEN?' A voice deep as a funeral bell, vibrating with power, beat back the sea around his ears.

All round him the singing died. The mermaids subsided silently, like the falling tide. They left a wide expanse of silver sand in the middle of which Pangur found himself all alone, struck still by that voice in the very act of flight. Some of the sailors began to sit up and watch.

'COME!' The voice boomed to him like the sea through hollow caves.

Unwillingly, Pangur's paws began to move. Small white paws, like daisies, picking themselves off the sandy floor, one by one, moving him forward, without his wanting them to. Far, far ahead of him on a coral-crusted rock, a blood-red shadow moved.

'COME CLOSER.'

It was too far for comfort. A huge arena of sand to cross alone, watched by all those eyes.

'COME HERE!' The Sea Witch leaned down from the amethyst throne of Ancofva.

She was ancient, terrible, and beautiful. A face on which time had hollowed the flesh from the bones, like runnels carved by flowing water on rock. Hair, grey as rain-clouds in September dusk. Her breasts gleamed like old ivory and her tail was antique silver, coiled under her, with the great forked fins springing free. Rose-red, blood-red, those fins. Stirring the sand as they twitched, ever so gently.

'NOW! LOOK AT ME!'

He raised his pointed face to hers, and the emerald eyes, cold as a frozen waterfall, sharper than stars, skewered his brain and severed his memory.

Then, 'Martin?' A stumbling voice wavered behind him.

49

'Did you say *Martin*?'

Niall was staggering to his feet. The Sea Witch blinked in astonishment. Pangur spun round as her eyes released him. And suddenly he remembered what he must do. He wasn't going to come to her and he wasn't going to stay. He was going to go!

'Niall! Follow me!'

And he fled, bounding straight through the shoal of startled mermaids. Away from the danger that he knew, away from those blinding eyes and the spells of the mermaids, out into the infinity of the ocean.

'KILL HIM! CATCH THE EARTHCAT AND KILL HIM!' her voice tolled behind him. 'THE SPELL IS WEAKENING!'

He hadn't time to see if Niall was following him. As the hollow death-knell of her voice pursued him he gave a startled yell and tumbled off the shelving ledge of shore. Over and over he went, down into the deep, dim hollows of the sea. Then he was away, swimming frantically through the chill twilight. Deeper and deeper, down into the swaying kelp.

For a moment he looked up. Dark shapes were diving over his head. Twisting, hunting relentlessly. He was scuttling over dark weed now, like a small white octopus, wishing he was any other colour. The shadows blurred and went, and came and blurred and went above him. He heard them calling to each other like baying hounds.

Cold water raced over his head. In a blue-black whirlpool the great tail lashed and turned. A face white as the moon in front of his. He struggled to turn. The inescapable hands shot out and closed around him. He felt himself lifted up and his life faltered for a heartbeat.

The sad blue eyes of a merman looked down at him with surprise.

'Why!' he said. 'I know what you are. You're a *cat*!'

11

Pangur squirmed desperately. 'Let me go! I wasn't doing any harm! Please let me go!'

But the merman stared down at him and said slowly, 'But what is a *cat* doing under the sea?'

'I'm a very *small* cat. Not dangerous,' Pangur said hastily. 'Anyway, how did you know I was a cat? Morwenna said she'd never caught one before.'

The merman's face softened with the memory of a dream. 'It was not here. I've seen men, and dogs, even horses here, but not cats. That was in Kernow, three hundred years ago, in a village of Earthmen . . . and Earthmaids.'

The hands were slackening. A few moments more and Pangur would be able to spring for freedom.

'And what would a merman be doing in a village of Earth?'

'Singing, of course. It is what we were made for. Oh, we sing too, like the mermaids, you know. Only our songs are to women. And there are not many of those that come riding the sea. Always it is Earthmen. Sailors, fishermen, merchants, warriors. Sailing the deep or walking too near the shore at night. They hear the mermaids calling. And they follow them. Out, and under, and down, to the palaces under the sea. And they forget the Earth they left. But always men. If mermen would find Earthmaids, we must go to them.'

'And did you find one? Did she follow you?' Flexing his body gently under the fingers.

'I saw her walking on the beach and sang to her. She heard my calling. For the first time in seven hundred years an Earthmaid heard the voice of Gwynion and started to follow. Small white feet over the seaweed. Oh, such feet! You can't imagine. With pink, round toe-nails! And ankles above each foot, and white calves, soft-skinned, with golden down!' He was like a hungry beggar describing a feast he had once glimpsed.

'And then?' Pangur eased his shoulders free and gathered his muscles.

Gwynion's head drooped. 'There was a sound of church bells chiming. She turned and listened. Then she began to clamber back to the shore. I followed through the rocks, singing with all my heart. But my song was no more to her than the sighing of the wind, against that bell. She sat down on the beach and put on her stockings and shoes, and went to church.

'Now it was I who followed her. The Earth is very painful for us, but I did not care. I heaved myself up a beach of stones, and over the road, and up the path to the church. It was better for me there. Cool stone, bare wood. And the singing of Earthmen and Earthwomen. At the end of the mass she turned and saw me. And she smiled.

'For a year and a day I followed her to church. She smiled and loved me. At last she promised that on New Year's Eve she would come to me at the shore and take hold of my hand, and dive with me down to the palace under the sea for ever.'

'But she didn't come?'

'I never saw her again. On New Year's Eve the Sea Witch raised a storm. The waves hurled themselves upon the shore. The fishing boats were smashed. The sea swept up into the houses and destroyed them. It rushed into the church and the tower came tumbling down and the bell with it. All the people were drowned, or fled into the hills. My Earthmaid never came back. But a great ship was wrecked that night. A hundred men, princes and warriors, came down into our realm. All men. The Sea Witch is afraid of Earthwomen. They have the power to make men remember the sky. So I shall never see my maid again. The Sea Witch will never allow an Earthmaid under the sea. She fears their power.'

The restless cat grew suddenly very still.

'But there is one here now.'

'Where? She has come at last? Oh, *where*?'

Pangur wriggled in the clutching hands.

'Oh, not yours, I'm afraid. She couldn't be, after all this time. But she's a real Earthmaid, all the same. You know. Feet, toenails, ankles, everything. Just like you said.'

'Oh, if I could only see her! If I could sing to her. Just to remember!'

'You'd better be quick then. She's in mortal danger. Morwenna trussed her up like a hunter's kill, and something very nasty has got her now. It may be eating her already. But what could I do? I'm a very *small* cat. And this was something under the mud, something huge, with a forest of tentacles, and great red eyes, and I shouldn't wonder if it had a great red mouth as well, but I didn't wait to see.'

The merman dropped Pangur, leaving him hanging spreadeagled in the water. A shudder ran down the blue-black tail.

'The Pengoggen! They have given the Earthmaid to *him*!'

'I'm afraid so. Oh, is it too late? Will he have eaten her already? I went to get help as fast as I could. I found Niall. But I couldn't rouse him. The mermaids have snared him in their song, like a salmon in a net. He can no more move than Finnglas can. I tried to break the spell. But there wasn't time.'

'It needs an Earthwoman to do that ...', said Gwynion slowly. 'That is why the mermaids fear all women. And this Earthmaid, you say ...'

'Is trapped and trussed in the Pengoggen's lair! Oh, is there no way out! Can't you help? Will she die? Is she dead already?'

'The Pengoggen feasts when sun and moon stand face to face, and the flood tide rises to the springs.'

The merman seized the cat by the paw and sped to the surface. The satin water rippled gently without wind. The sun had turned past noon. Gwynion smiled grimly.

'It is full moon this evening. You have until nightfall.'

'Then she's still alive?' Hope surged within Pangur for the first time. 'You can save her?'

'I?' The smile faded from the merman's face. 'What can

I do? The only magic I have is in my voice. And you'd hardly expect the Pengoggen to fall for *me*.'

'But who has the magic? The Sea Witch . . .'

'The Sea Witch would see her dead.'

'Then it's no use? We just sit here and wait for Finnglas to be eaten alive? That's horrible! Oh, I wish I was home! *Think*, Gwynion! An Earthmaid, here! There must be *something* you can do.'

'I do not have the power . . . No, wait, little cat! There *is* hope yet. A thousand years ago I heard tell of one whose knowledge is greater than either of them. Wiser than the Sea Witch. Older even than the Pengoggen. When the world was young, and the rocks were new-formed from the ocean, and the Pengoggen's lair was an eyrie in the mountains, even then she was swimming.'

'Yes, yes! Who is she?'

'The Wisest One of all. The Salmon Hen.'

'*Where* is she?'

'A thousand years ago she was at the bottom of the pool of the hazel trees.'

'*What* hazel trees?'

'In the pool of the hazel trees, at the head of the river, under the snows of Plynlimmon.'

'Plynlimmon!' Anger shook the white cat. 'You're playing games with me! That must be hundreds of miles across sea and land. How do you think I could get to the mountain and back before the moon rises?'

'You are luckier than you know, little cat. She lies in Ancofva, the Place of Forgetting. One hour with the mermaids is a month on Earth. You may yet be in time.'

'But I can't swim. Not properly, anyway. I'm only a small cat, not a dog. How can I get to Plynlimmon?'

'Whistle the wind.'

Gwynion put his fingers to his lips and whistled to the four corners of the ocean, spinning round like an autumn leaf in a gale. There was a moment's silence. Then the sea grew dark beneath them. It began to boil. Whirlpools. Waves. Rollers. Breakers. A white tempest was flying towards them before the gale. White manes streaming along green necks.

The flash of rolling eyes. Sides slippery, tossing, bucketing. A herd of wild sea-horses. Galloping past Pangur and the merman. Jostling them. Bucking beneath them, as though they were stray flecks of foam.

Gwynion stroked their smooth flanks as they raced past, and ran his fingers through their tumbling white manes.

'Sweet horses, gentle horses,' he said soothingly. 'Will you carry Pangur Bán?'

'Whei-i-i,' they whinnied, stamping and turning in the tossing spray. Their nostrils flared. 'We did not come because you called. We will not go where you say. We race the wind.'

'Where do you run?'

'To the limits of the ocean. Till the rocks resist us or we stumble in the sand.'

'Then carry Pangur Bán to the great river of Albion. The oldest river. To the source of all. For the sake of an Earthmaid he seeks the Wise One, the Salmon Hen, in the pool under the hazel trees in the shadow of Plynlimmon.'

'For what should we carry him?'

'For the love of galloping. For the width of the sea. For the speed of your youth.'

'For that we will go,' said their leader. 'Not for you. Not for the Earthcat. Not for the maid. Because we are free and owe nothing to anyone. We will go. If he rides with us, it is one. And if he stays, it is the same. The horses of Manawyddan go galloping.'

'Mount, little Earthcat,' said the merman. 'They wait for no one. But do not hold them. Do not try to govern them. Let your spirit gallop with theirs. If you fear, you will fall and they will trample you under their hooves. But if you trust yourself to them, they will carry you to the ends of the ocean and your heart's desire. No one rules them but the Sea Witch, and even she with difficulty. Pray with all your soul that the wave of your going does not reach her under the sea. Good luck!'

'But you? Aren't you coming with me?'

'An Earthmaid, you said ...?' His violet eyes began to shine. 'Lying in the lair of the Pengoggen? A real Earthmaid?'

'Definitely. With toe-nails.'

In a sudden burst of resolution, Gwynion cried, 'Then I will dare to find her!' He slapped the flank of the leader of the sea-horses.

'Away!' he cried, and his eyes were laughing recklessly.

'Away!' thundered the sea-stallion. 'Not because you say, but because the wind is running. Away to the shores of Earth and the mother of oceans. To the mouth of the River Severn!'

With a wild cry, bearing Pangur on their backs, they galloped away over the surface of the ocean, whitening the waves like driven hail. The storm of their going shivered down through the depths. If the Sea Witch had not been quivering with fury, she would have felt it.

The last faint tremor of their passing stirred the mud in the brown depths of the Pengoggen's lair.

12

Finnglas opened her eyes. She could see nothing. It was very cold, very still, very quiet. For a while she lay trembling in the darkness, trying to ward off the memory of those hungry red eyes, that sucking noise, the cavernous mouth dribbling over her ...

Her hand tried to grope, longing for the hilt of Cruimthan. But she could not move it. Her fingers seemed to be stuck together with slime.

'Pangur Bán! Niall! Help me!' Finnglas tried to shout. Her lips would not move. Something was covering her mouth. She twisted and turned. Even her eyes seemed veiled.

It was very dark. Cloudy. Every movement was a struggle. Something worse than Morwenna's rope was binding her now. Closing her lips, her eyelashes, her nostrils. Clogging the very skin of her face into a set pattern that she could not change. Sticking her arms to her sides. She felt a thick sea-slime, like jelly, slowly setting round her.

'Mmmm!' She writhed and twisted. But the movements were getting harder every moment.

'Help!' she tried to call. The sound vibrated in her throat and got no further. Her lips would not open.

She lay back, exhausted. Silence was thick about her in the gloom.

'One. Two. Three. Four. Five,' said a small, brisk voice.

'Where did I get to? One, two, three, four, five, six ... No, wrong again. *One,* two, three, four, five ... What's over this way? One, two, three, four, five, five and a half ... Five and a *half*?'

Through the streaked veil of slime across her eyes Finnglas saw a small gleam of green light hurry sideways to her and stop. A tiny crab hopped over her legs, the points of its claws piercing the slime so that it tickled unbearably. It danced up to her head and back to her toes.

'Five and three-quarters? Oh, call it six, though it's a good deal smaller than usual. We shall just have to hope his Unpleasantness isn't feeling too peckish this month.'

'Help! Please, help me!' Finnglas tried to shout. But all that came through her sticky lips was a groan.

The crab scuttled backwards and fell off her knees into the mud.

'Oh, dear! Oh, dear! That is ... His most Merciful, most Benevolent, the all-Loving, his most Smiling and Adorable Highness ... Oh, it's you, my dear. I thought for a moment it was ... Oh, well, never mind.'

'Mmmm!' Finnglas struggled to speak.

'It's no good. You'd better save your breath. You can't talk, you know. That stuff will be set as hard as a skate's egg-case by moonrise. I'd better get these ropes off while there's still time. Very indigestible stuff, rope. He wouldn't like it at all. And if *He* doesn't like it ... Oh, dear; oh, my!'

The tiny claws bit busily into the ropes. Finnglas felt the pain in her wrists and ankles slacken. In a wild burst of energy she struggled to sit up.

'It's no good, you know,' said the crab reprovingly. 'Or I wouldn't have taken the ropes away. His slime is much better and not nearly so painful. In a little while you won't even be able to move.'

'I *can't* move!' Finnglas moaned incomprehensibly.

'Now, where was I? One, two, three, four, five, six. Seven? Is there a seven in the house? No? Well, really, the mermaids will have to do better than this, or we shall all pay for it. Not a full larder, and the sun going down already. Dear me, the Sea Witch had better hear of this. If she can't keep him properly fed, there'll be trouble. And don't tell me she can't spare some of her own catch. I've heard them singing. A fine, jolly fisherman, now. Or a monk. Did somebody say she had caught a monk? It's a long time since his Repulsiveness had one of those. But I remember a time when three of them came down. Two were nothing but poles and string, but the third . . . he must have been a fine, beer-swilling fellow. Oh, he went down particularly well. His Hideousness slept for a week. A whole week, without stirring from the mud, and those great red eyes of his shut like clams. Oh, the joy of it. The relief of it. A monk! I hope this one's fat as well . . .'

The voice went chittering away and was lost in the mud.

'Help! Don't leave me!' Finnglas moaned. But already she was afraid of what her groans might waken next.

'Niall?' she tried to whisper.

No one answered.

Then, less hopefully, 'Pangur Bán?'

The silence settled deeper than before. The water was very cold.

It would be easier to sleep. Relax her clenched muscles. Let go her stiffening eyelids. Stop striving for breath. As the Pengoggen's vile juices hardened round her, she need never wake again. When the full moon rose he would suck the life from her body and gnaw her flesh, and she would not know. She could let go. She could die. Now. Peacefully.

No! She kicked angrily with her ankles. It did little good. She could not escape. But she was alive. She was fighting. She would go on fighting to the end. Struggling against the sickness of terror, she made herself remember. Those groping tentacles, blinding her face, tangling in her hair, had sucked her backwards. So the way out must lie beyond her feet. With a last effort she started to heave herself in that direction.

Her knees would scarcely bend. Her slime-coated heels slipped and slipped endlessly in the mud. And all the time she was terrified that the Pengoggen might feel her under the sea-bed. But when there was no breath left in her caked nostrils she had still pushed herself no nearer to safety than the length of her own head. She fell back, unable even to pant.

A great, dark shadow came swimming over her. She shut her eyes tightly.

'Earthmaid?'

Now she could not even open her eyes to see her end.

'Mmmm!'

A pressure on her arm, faintly perceived through the smothering ooze. Touching her hair, her cheek. So gently. It was not the Pengoggen. Someone had found her.

She wanted to cry, 'Help me get out!'

'Earthmaid?'

She could barely hear now. But someone settled himself beside her and took her hand. He was trembling.

'I never thought to see another Earthmaid, not here, under the sea. It's been such a long time. You're not as beautiful as her, of course. The Earthcat was right. You have legs, ankles, feet. And I expect there are toenails inside those boots. Only ... well, I wouldn't have known you were a woman, if he hadn't said. I'd have thought you were a warrior. But ... well, I can see now you're not. And you wouldn't be here if you were, would you? You'd be up under the sunshine with the mermaids, with Morwenna. Only ... they couldn't risk an Earthwoman, you see. You're too dangerous. All those Earthmen. You might break the spell that holds them.

'I shouldn't be here, you know. If the ... If *He* were to smell me ... He's eaten mermen before. Even the Sea Witch couldn't stop him. And if *she* knew ... But I don't care. I had to see you once, before you died.'

'Help me!' Finnglas tried to say.

'There! Don't try to talk. You can't, you know. By tonight you won't be able to hear or see or feel. The slime turns black. Black and hard. It must be dreadful. But he won't eat you just yet. He'll keep you till the moon has risen and the tide is full and his belly is empty. And then the great feast will begin. Unless Pangur Bán finds ...'

'Pangur?' Finnglas gave a smothered cry.

'Ssh!' Gwynion gripped her hand in terror. 'He'll hear you! If he should wake and find me ... Oh, but it's a shame. Such little fingers ... A real Earthmaid. I wonder! Would I dare? While he's asleep ... could I carry you ...?'

'Yes! Yes!' Finnglas moaned.

She felt his arms sliding under her through the mud. She felt him lifting her towards the opening. Towards life.

Then with a cry of anguish he dropped her and leapt

back. As she fell on to the sea-bed Finnglas felt it heave beneath her. Currents of mud rushed past her face, choking her. She could not turn to see the nightmare that was coming behind her. But her dimmed eyes saw two huge red patches like charcoal fires burn on the white of Gwynion's chest. With a yell and a sweep of his great fins he turned and dived into the passage. The red light scorched his vanishing tail.

A loathsome mouth groped over Finnglas, dribbling.

13

The brilliant blue sky rushed overhead. Clouds fiercely, joyously white, and the foam of the sea-horses' manes too bright to look at. Pangur stood poised on the stallion's back, like a small scud of spray, astonished, incredibly enjoying himself. Air rushed into his saturated lungs and his soft white fur began to dry in the sun. How could he be so happy when Finnglas lay close to death?

Through the billows rushing towards him came a picture of stillness. Martin. Lying on the floor. Red paint dripping from the table. Blood flowing, trickling, stopping. Martin. Dead. And Finnglas, his sister, bound and still, in terrible darkness. The cold of his wet toes on the stallion's back crept up into his heart.

'Faster,' he cried to the stallion. 'Faster!'

The horses of Manawyddan did not need his urging. The sunlit sea-herd swept on to the coast of Kernow and of Cymru. Past Lundy and Llanteilo, Mor Hafren and Cair Gwent. On, on up the Severn. Crowded together now, manes merging in a long white roller, shining backs piled upon one another, a mounting, rearing, towering wall of horses rushed up the river, with Pangur, tail stiff and streaming, perched on its very crest.

Scouring the banks, drowning the reed beds, flooding the fields. On they rushed around the flanks of bellowing cows, till the bright sea dwindled behind them, and the green fields closed about them, and the river grew small and shallow, and their long joy was spent.

The stallion hung his head, panting.

'It is enough. The green land has swallowed our strength. We must go to the wind that made us, to the ocean and the gales. Go on up the river, little Earthcat, or return with us. It is all one to us. The horses of Manawyddan go. For the joy and the freedom and the circling of the earth.'

Pangur slipped off on to the stones. The cool water ran singing over his paws.

'Aren't you taking me all the way?'

'Do not ask. Do not expect. We will not be bound. Take what help you can, where you can, and be joyful. Look, the salmon are running.'

And they turned and cantered back down the river-bed, a shining, jostling herd, shaking their tails in the sun.

Pangur climbed out on to the bank and looked about him. Far, far away stood the blue-headed mountains. He was still a long way from Plynlimmon. And Finnglas was a long way behind him, and he was further than ever from home. Small and lost, he sat down and began to lick the salt from his fur.

But the water was not empty yet. Long, grey shapes came weaving up the river. Pangur watched them pressing forward against the falling current until they reached a weir. Then they raced forward. Silver bodies arched out of the water, leaping, falling, slithering back again. They rushed the weir a second time. Pangur padded up the bank to watch more closely. One by one, with enormous effort, they shot into the air, until with a last great leap they reached the pool above the weir and swam on out of sight.

Pangur sat down again wearily. If it was so hard for them to climb the river alone, how could they ever carry him on their backs? Yet how could he walk all that way on his tiny white paws and his small white legs? In Ancofva the day was dying, and on Earth it was autumn already.

He watched one salmon, greater than the rest, clear the weir in one bound and dive thankfully into the green, broad depths above. Pangur dipped a paw into the cloudy water.

'Excuse me . . .'

The salmon's eye glided past him incuriously.

'Excuse me. I've got to get to Plynlimmon. It's very urgent. It's . . . well, it's the sister of . . . well, it's Finnglas. It's a matter of life and death. I've got to get help for her. And Gwynion said, a thousand years ago, in the pool of the hazels under Plynlimmon . . . And I wondered . . . of course, I'd get off at the waterfalls. I could manage those on my own. But not the whole way. There isn't time.'

The salmon swam steadily on. Its sad voice floated back to him.

'I swim where I swim because she calls me. If you cased me in lead, and hung a stone round my neck, and chained my tail to a ball of iron, still I would try to swim the Severn to reach her. I go because I must. If I launched myself at a waterfall and fell back a hundred times, still I would leap the hundredth and first time. I have no choice. I climb the river because I must. In drought or flood, in sickness or in health, free or encumbered, I swim, and only death can stop me.'

'Does that mean yes?' asked Pangur doubtfully. 'Will you take me?'

'I swim because I must. I leap because there is no other way. With you or without you I must climb the Severn.'

For the last moment Pangur hesitated, but it was all the help there was. Reluctantly he slipped again into the cold river. As his claws hooked in the silver scales the salmon dived, powering through the shadowed pools, the streaming weed, the bubbling current, up, up . . . As they hurtled towards the waterfall, Pangur tumbled off and swam coughing to the stones. Blindly the salmon charged, slithering, writhing desperately between the rocks. Long before it succeeded, Pangur had clambered up the sunny grass and was sitting at the head of the waterfall, waiting anxiously. As the salmon reappeared, he mounted, and they were off again.

Day after day they forced their way up the river. As he clung to the great salmon, Pangur tried not to think of convent suppers, the steaming platters of fish with sweet juice running from the flesh. Martin feeding him titbits.

Both cat and salmon grew thin and hungry on the journey. Mile after mile, always struggling upwards, with the sun setting earlier every night. The river twisted north and west, into the very heart of the land, the birthplace of waters, till the shadow of Plynlimmon fell cold and blue across the pools.

At last, where the shale swept down to the water's edge,

and the first snow lingered in the hollows, the salmon slowed and sighed and stopped.

For a moment Pangur stayed where he was, too dazed to move. He could not believe that he had arrived. He had been carried so far. He did not want to stand on his own four feet again and have to act.

Then he remembered why he had come. He slipped sideways from the salmon and climbed out of the water.

'Thank you,' he said hesitantly.

There was no answer. All round him the salmon lay exhausted on the stones, their force spent, their journey over, seeming empty of life. He looked at them sadly. Would they feel, would they laugh again when they had spawned in the pools of their birthplace and the ocean called? Would the great run down the river find them joyous, carefree, bounding down the falls? He could not stay to see. Already he might be too late. How long had Finnglas lain bound in the Pengoggen's lair? Could she really live until the full moon rose? Was Gwynion sure?

'The Wise One? The Salmon Hen? Where is she?' he asked.

The salmon lay as if dead. All around him was silence, except for the trickling of a thin waterfall down which the young river tumbled. It seemed to fall from rocks against the sky. He clambered up it. It was higher and harder than any he had climbed before, and he was weak with hunger. He stopped on its crest, blinking and tottering.

He was looking down into the source of all, the first pool. It was guarded by trees. Old, spreading, knotted. Pointing their sharp brown fingers at the water. The banks under their leaves were silent, still.

The water was black. No ripple stirred its surface. But it was not empty. Pangur was sure of that.

He took a step cautiously downwards. A breeze rustled the grass. The hair on his neck stood stiffly upright.

He reached the trees, stepping carefully over the hazel-roots. The wind shivered the branches. Under the leaves, the nuts rustled against each other.

He came to the edge of the water. Silence. His own

reflection, small and white in the circle of black. He waited. Silence.

Pangur sat down and began to wash, nervously.

'Wise One?' he called presently. His tongue felt dry.

But there was only the wind shaking the leaves so that the hazel nuts fell into the water.

He thought of Morwenna, casting her cowrie shells to the Pengoggen. But he had nothing to offer.

Dry grass heads rustled against his legs. He gathered their seeds and crushed them into flour and scattered it on the water.

'Salmon Hen?'

Silence.

Feeling rather foolish he got up and looked around. White clover starred the grass beyond the trees. He picked a flowerhead and carried it to the water's edge. With his paw he squeezed each stamen. The golden nectar dripped into the water.

'Wisest One?'

Silence.

He sat down and thought. At last he scooped his paw into the crinkles of his ear. He tasted it with his pink tongue, and nodded, satisfied. After a week's journey he carried still the crusted salt of the sea.

But his paw hovered, uneasily, over the surface of the pool. So black, so quiet. He did not want to wake it.

But he had come for this. Trembling, he dipped his paw into the dark depths and drew it back quickly. At once a great ripple broke the surface. Spreading, shining, rolling. Pangur sprang back. The wave washed up the bank, lapping his feet. A hoary head had risen out of the pool. A huge silver and black eye looked at him thoughtfully.

'Yes?'

'Yes!' said Pangur rapidly. 'Oh, yes. I mean ... It's me, Pangur Bán. That is ... Hail, Wise One ...' His nose went hot and pink.

'Yes?' said the Salmon Hen unblinkingly.

Before her gaze, he felt his need come loose like an ice-bound stream in springtime.

66

'I called you. But it's not me really. It's Finnglas. The Pengoggen's got her. In the mud beneath the sea. And he's going to eat her at nightfall. And winter is almost here so it must be nearly night in Ancofva. And the Sea Witch has got Niall, and hundreds of prisoners, and I can't wake him from the spell. And none of them will come and rescue Finnglas . . . He's got great red eyes, and thousands of arms! And Niall wouldn't come!'

'No?' The water trembled slightly.

'Oh, you don't understand! It's because I killed Martin. It was all my fault. And Drusticc said we must redeem each drop of blood with someone's life. And Finnglas is his sister. That's why she tried to kill me. Oh, she mustn't die too!'

The deep voice eddied round him reassuringly.

'Do not fear. Finnglas can save Niall.'

'But you haven't been listening! I want Niall to save *Finnglas*!' He was almost crying.

'Why? Finnglas is dying. But Niall is bewitched.'

'But she's bound with ropes. She's in his lair. He's going to *eat* her!'

'All things must die.'

'Then you won't save her? But Gwynion said . . . Then I've come all this way for *nothing*!'

'The sea-horses were galloping, and you rode with them. The salmon were running, and you swam with them. These things are not given to every cat. Were they nothing?'

'But that's not what I wanted! It's not for myself. It's for Finnglas! *Can't* you help?'

The eye rolled over and sank beneath the surface. The wind shook the hazel trees and the nuts floated out on the water like small brown boats. The deep voice rose singing from the depths.

'Beneath the sea,
She lies afraid.
Beneath the stone,
She lies alone.

What holds her now
Encased in death

67

No fire can melt
But Arthmael's breath.

Beneath the wave
He breaks death's grip.
Beneath the stone,
Arthmael alone.'

'Arthmael?' said Pangur desperately. 'Who's Arthmael?'
The ripples broke, revealing half a bright eye.
'Arthmael is joy.'
'But *where* is Arthmael?'
'Playing, of course. With those I have made for play.
With the selkies, in the sea beyond Iona.'
'Iona? Where's *that*?'
'West of the Picts. East of the Scots. The most holy
island of the Hebrides.'
'But I haven't got *time*!' cried Pangur. 'She'll be dead by
then!'
And he buried his face in his paws.

For the last time the voice echoed from the depths of the pool and rang round the sky.

'*Ask. Expect.*'

Pangur lifted his head from his paws.

'Do you mean you *can*? You can! Please, *help me!*'

The day turned golden in front of his eyes. A wall of gold. A mountain of gold. A whirlwind of gold. He leapt backwards. A golden eagle landed on the rock in front of him.

Pangur crouched trembling before the curved talons. A small white cat would be only a mouthful for that beak.

'Who summons me?' the harsh voice cried.

'I ... I think I must have done. Who are you?'

'The Lord of the Air. Mynio Mighty-Grasp. I fly over Mon, over Man, over Mull. To where the waters wash the western isles, and Columcille feeds the birds of heaven.'

The words dropped at Pangur's feet waiting for him to pick them up.

'And ... where is that?'

'The holy island. To Iona.'

'Then did you ... have you ever heard of Arthmael?'

The eagle vaulted into the sky, turned a somersault against the sun, and landed in front of Pangur in a flurry of gold.

'*Heard* of Arthmael? *Heard* of him? Are there those who have not!'

'Could you ... would you take me with you?'

'Come!'

Mynio Mighty-Grasp spread enormous pinions at full stretch, muscles soaking up the sunshine, feathers fanned against the light. Wondering at his own daring, Pangur stepped between his shoulders and shut his eyes as the huge bird soared into the sky. Above the mountain peaks of Cymru they spiralled upwards, catching the winds of heaven. Then, like an arrow, their arching flight sped into the north. The summer sea spread an embroidery of islands below them, their silvered shores stitched with threads of foam.

'Will it really be all right?' called Pangur to Mynio. 'Will Arthmael save her in time? Can it be this easy after all?'

'Nothing worthwhile is easy,' shouted Mynio. 'It is not easy to nest on the peaks of mountains. It is not easy to ride the hurricane. It is not easy to hunt and to be hunted. But it is glorious.'

They plunged suddenly downwards and landed on a low, green, grassy island. Grey boulders, hummocks of buildings, a haze of smoke.

A monk in a white robe watched them descend. He started in surprise as Pangur tumbled off into the grass.

'What have we here? Puss! Puss! Puss!' he called, holding out his hand.

Pangur looked at him doubtfully. Painful memories stirred at the sight of the monk.

'Here, little brother.'

Stiff-legged with weariness, Pangur made a shaky step towards him.

'Will you look at the bones sticking out of him? Don't be afraid. We have milk in the kitchen. Fresh fish. Bread. Come, little one.'

Hunger roared in Pangur's belly. Saliva rushed to his mouth. The savoury smell of the cooking fire drifted towards him.

It brought back memories. Of Martin, feeding him bread and fish. Martin, now dead. And Martin's sister, Finnglas . . .

In a tiny plaintive mew he whispered, 'I must find Arthmael.'

It was like shutting the door in his own face. He turned his head away from the food-scented smoke, and swallowed hard.

The monk's face softened. He picked up the little cat.

'So thin. And so brave. The need must be very great, little brother. Come with me.'

He carried Pangur down to the shore and out over the stones to the last ledge. Then he laid him down on the warm rock in the sunshine.

'Wait,' he said. 'And hope.'

He shaded his eyes with his hand and stared out to sea. Then he went away smiling.

Far out to sea the waves lifted over the reefs. Lifted and fell. And in and out of their sparkling sides grey heads were lifting and falling, diving and reappearing. A long dark shape shot out of the water, arching across the sky and fell with a splash. Pangur blinked in the sunshine.

Beside him the waves lifted against the rocks. Lifted and fell. With all the weariness of travelling and the lightness of hunger, Pangur felt himself drifting away. Lifting and falling. As though the stone was rocking in the sea.

A cold wave splashed into his face. He opened his eyes and leapt back. The great, black and white, bottle-nosed, bulbous, fish-eyed, laughable face of a dolphin rose out of the sea in front of him. The clown's eyes twinkled.

'Hello. Are you playing?'

Pangur gulped back his disappointment.

'Please! Can you help me? I'm looking for Arthmael.'

'Would you like to see me do a backward somersault?'

With a great swish of his tail, the dolphin leapt out of the water and toppled backwards in a cloud of spray.

'Oh, please! Be serious. I've come such a very long way. Do you know where he is?'

'Can you dance? I can dance on my tail. Watch this.'

He dived, streaming under the water, shot through the surface up into the sunshine. Slap, slap, slap went his tail, skittering over the waves. He fell with a heavy splash, drenching Pangur.

'Stop it! Stop it!' wailed Pangur desperately.

'What do I have to do to make you laugh? Shall I sing to you?'

'No! Go away! I don't want you.'

'You've hurt my feelings.'

71

'I want Arthmael.'

The dolphin stormed up to the rock and lay suddenly still. Only two sparkling eyes and an open blow-hole showed. From deep underwater the name came bubbling up.

'*Pangur Bán!*'

The loving laughter in his voice shook the whole sea. And Pangur understood.

'You! *You* are Arthmael?'

The dolphin's face twinkled, 'Watch me!'

Then he turned and dived. Leaping, diving. In and out of the waves like a skimming slate. In a swirl of foam he was coming back. Out of the water, up on his fluked tail, skittering, running, dancing on the sunlit sea. In a mighty fountain of spray he dived to the bottom, wetting Pangur again, and rose bubbling to the surface.

'Yes! *I am Arthmael*!' he cried.

'Then, please,' begged Pangur, wet and weary. 'Can you help me? The Salmon Hen sent me to you. The Wise One, in the pool of the hazels, under Plynlimmon. It's Finnglas. The Pengoggen . . .'

'I can't hear a word you're saying. Your belly's rumbling.' And Arthmael vanished.

Pangur sat down. The sea seemed suddenly colder, and the sun had dimmed a little.

Then, in a flurry of spray, Arthmael was back.

'Here! Have a sprat!'

A wet fish struck him on the nose. Pangur shot out a paw with claws unsheathed.

'Why don't you *listen*! Finnglas is dying . . .'

'It's rude to talk with your mouth full,' mumbled Arthmael, opening his jaws and spilling a scatter of wriggling sprats upon the stone.

'Now, eat!' he shouted. 'And be thankful!'

Pangur looked down. The small, live fish were right beneath his nose. His mouth watered unbearably. The temptation was too much. His jaws crunched blissfully on the food. He ate on. His sides began to swell and his throat slowed.

Suddenly, with a whisk of his flippers, Arthmael swept

72

the rest of the fish from under his nose. The sprats fell back into the sea in a silver rain.

'That's enough,' he said. And to the sprats he shouted, 'Go! And be thankful! Now, you were saying . . .?'

'It's Finnglas,' stuttered Pangur, swallowing the last mouthful. 'She's . . .'

'At last!' cried Arthmael, leaping out of the water and knocking him backwards. 'I thought you'd never ask!'

'Then you . . .'

'What are you waiting for? Christmas?'

'You mean you'll come with me?'

The black and white face rose out of the waves and stared mischievously into his.

'Don't you think,' Arthmael asked gently, 'it would be quicker if *you* came with *me*?'

The great dolphin lay still and waiting. Pangur stepped nervously on to his glistening back. Of all the steeds he had mounted in his quest, this was the most dangerous. No mane to grasp, no feathered shoulders, not even the ribbed scales of the salmon between his legs. He felt himself slipping helplessly.

'Are you afraid, Pangur Bán?'

'N-no . . . Oh! Yes!'

'Good. You would be a fool if you were not. And I am fool enough for all the world. Let go, and trust me!'

The dolphin's beak tossed sharply. Pangur squawked as he felt himself catapulted into the air. He was falling now. Below him were grinning jaws, rows of teeth. With a snap, Arthmael caught him in his mouth and the jaws closed round him like a palisade.

'Whatever you do, don't tickle,' muttered Arthmael through clenched teeth. 'If you make me laugh, I'll be the death of you. And now, to Finnglas!'

With a great whistle of breath, he plunged for the south.

Pangur lay cradled in the soft ridges of Arthmael's mouth, looking out at the ocean through the grinning teeth. The streaming tentacles of squid shot past, the fierce eyes of sharks. Startled jellyfish wobbled out of their headlong path. All day they drove through sparkling shoals of mackerel. As night fell they went powering past phosphorescent eyes. When the dawn broke, a new day burst upon his sight like fire in a cavern of emeralds.

Could they save Finnglas? He lay helpless, watching the world flash past through Arthmael's smile.

15

Niall let his eyes wander sleepily. The sunlit sea swam before him, as though he saw it through a haze of beer. Pale green, gilded with bubbles in the dying sun. Morwenna, bright as a kingfisher, swept past him, so that the waves stroked his shoulders. A rainbow-coloured troupe of mermaids streaked after her. So fast they swam. So purposeful. Their minds bent wholly on the magic they were weaving. They broke the surface of the sea, twined themselves on the reefs, and began to sing. From far above their voices chimed like bells in a high tower. Slow, sleepy smiles spread over the faces of the men, and they settled themselves more comfortably against the rocks of the sea-bed.

'Martin ...?' murmured Niall with a puzzled frown. 'Who was Martin?'

Morwenna swam down, and twined her fingers lovingly through his half-shaved hair.

'Remember me,' she murmured. 'Forget the Earth, and only remember me.'

The songs came showering down through the sea upon him like a silver waterfall, washing him clean of memories.

Not a tremor of their music came down to the dark depths where Finnglas lay. Long ago all sound had ceased for her. As the Pengoggen's juices hardened about her, choking her senses, she was on the edge of despair.

'I can't breathe!' she thought, fighting for life. 'I shall die. Even before he eats me. I shall die *now*!'

And then she wondered. 'I have breathed air. And I have breathed water. Perhaps I can learn to live without breathing at all.'

Her chest fell still. She let the silence fill her ears. Her blinded eyes relaxed. Slowly, concentrating all her being, she turned her life inward ...

There was a meadow, in midsummer, where the tall grass-heads curled soft as feathers, ruffled by the breeze. She was walking with someone, swishing, swishing up the hill. The long skyline was black against the brightness of the sky. They reached the top. The world lay before them. Blue and white in the morning, with the river winding its way into the distance. A group of men was waiting by the road.

She turned to her brother. 'Martin! You will come back to us, won't you?'

He took her hand, warm, loving. 'Little sister,' he said. 'I go now where the wind of God blows me. Perhaps Drusticc the Abbess will steer me in your direction one day. Perhaps not. But it is all joy. We will never be parted. Remember that.'

And he broke free from her and went down the hill to join the men. He wore the chequered breeches and the embroidered tunic of a king's son. But they would take the fine clothes from him. They would give him a robe of brown wool, and sandals for his tall leather boots. He had himself taken the golden torque from his neck, last night at the feasting, and given it back to his father. He would never be king. The monks and nuns would make him like one of them. And not like her. She was all the sons her father had now. She fingered the gold at her throat.

She stood and watched him go, waving from the hilltop. Straight and firm, determined not to cry. Then the dust swallowed him at the bend of the road and she could turn away.

She was blind with tears now, so that the sun danced darkly in her eyes. A rumpling breath quickened the skin of her face, and lifted her hair. Finnglas snatched back a sob and raised her head.

The piebald pony stood in front of her, pawing the poppies at her feet. The wind rippled the hair along its sides, islands of black and white. Its eyes shone with the promise of excitement. It leaned down the white blaze of its nose for her to caress. Its back invited her to mount . . .

In spite of herself, Finnglas writhed in her hard black coffin. Her lips were gummed together. She could not shout. Yet her still-speaking heart cried, 'Melisant!'

There was the first stab of feeling in her right leg. Finnglas went rigid with fear. Waking from memories into the nightmare of the present. She wanted to leap away, to spring to her feet, to run. But she could not move. She could not even open her eyes. She lay stiff and helpless, feeling the pain of life invading her leg, and knowing with horror what it meant.

For longer than she could remember she had been afraid of the cold numbness and the darkness. But now she wanted to snatch them back. Wanted to cling to the waiting, the stillness, the last shreds of living. Her nerves screamed as the growing heat crept up her leg.

And she could do nothing, nothing! She must lie here unmoving while that great horned mouth seared into her flesh like a torch. She would still be alive when the yellow teeth sank into her. Tearing. Devouring. How long would it last before she died, and what unbearable terror and pain yawned between this moment and death? If only she could fight!

There was a stickiness beginning to creep down the side of her leg now. The casing was melting back into slime. How hungry was the Pengoggen after his fast? Would he bite this leg off, now, as soon as it was free? Was that how death would begin? Or would he breathe over every part of her, slavering, slowly dissolving all his work, so that he could eat her body whole? Would she live long enough to feel his foul breath close upon her face? Would she open her eyes for the last time to see those fierce red eyes glaring hungrily into hers before the jaws opened? And she could not struggle! She could not even cry out!

Her hand had been lying useless by her side for so long that she had stopped thinking about it. But now the heat prickled in her fingertips, and she felt the softness of running slime. With dreadful excitement she knew that as his breath moved up her arm she would be able to move once more.

Her muscles tightened. If she were quick enough, could she strike with her fingernails at his red eyes? Could she tear them out, so that the two of them struggled blindly for her life? Or, at the first movement, would his curved teeth snap her arm off, and the swarming tentacles coil round her, holding her helpless to await the rest. How much longer dared she wait?

She kept very still. Her left leg was coming free. And her left arm. Now she felt the heat on her chest. She could breathe more easily. In a few moments he would reach her face. She could not bear it!

With a lunge of ferocious desperation she flung her arms upwards, finger-nails outspread, clawing, lashing, raking, her feet kicking at his underbelly. Her hands struck a huge, slippery face, but there was nothing to grasp, pain shooting up her stiff elbows, her arms too weak to hold. She felt her fingers slithering helplessly on the wet skin. She dug her nails in, and felt the flesh rip down the neckless body, skin tearing, blood running hot through her fingers.

She had lost. And now she must have enraged him. She sensed a huge body poised over hers. She tried to twist her head away.

The pain struck her left hand first. A row of sharp points, piercing her flesh. It was the beginning of the end. She waited for the jaws to close and the teeth to crunch through bone, leaving her mutilated. But the pain grew no worse. Pinpricks through the skin, like tiny claws. A weight settled on her wrist. Soft, damp fur. *Fur?*

Something else had her by the right arm now. It felt like grasping fingers. She kicked out wildly. The massive thing above her writhed, lashing her legs. Then its crushing weight descended on her and she could move no more.

Now the end *must* come, and she could only lie still and endure it.

His breath was on her neck. Hot. Prickling. Tickling. She felt she wanted to *laugh*.

80

Now her lips were coming free, her nostrils were breathing in and out, and her eyelids unsticking, lashes parting, the stickiness dissolving, rolling down her face, dripping away into the sea-bed, stray curls of her hair floating free.

'You stink!' said a high, unfamiliar voice. 'You need a bath.'

Her loosened eyes shot open. She was staring into smiling teeth, a bright, round eye, a ridiculous black and white snout.

Before she could find words, the ball of fur on her wrist squirmed. She twisted her stiff neck sideways.

'Pangur Bán!'

And on the other side, a merman, Gwynion, holding her hand and gazing at her with admiring eyes.

'I hope you don't mind,' apologized the dolphin. 'But I seem to be dripping blood all over you.'

Finnglas blinked her eyes hard. Even the sea-murk dazzled her unaccustomed sight. All down the dolphin's left side a deep furrow was scored. The skin hung in tatters and the flesh had been torn open. Blood dripped steadily down on to Finnglas's skin, her clothes, her hair, mingling with the last of the slime, dissolving it, washing it down into the mud. Finnglas closed her eyes and lay back speechless.

'Oh dear. She looks considerably weaker in life than she did in death. You'd better pick her up, Gwynion.'

'Is it safe now?'

'I shouldn't think so for a moment. Not *safe*. But it would be kind.'

The merman slipped his white arms cautiously around Finnglas. As he lifted her, they felt the sea-bed quiver.

'What was that?' Pangur gasped, the hair bristling on his neck.

'Only the Pengoggen. This is his home. I expect he's coming out to play.'

'*Play!*' miaowed Pangur, bolting for the passage. 'Come *on*!'

'Or dance,' said Arthmael. 'He should make a superb dancer, with all those legs. And Finnglas hasn't seen me

81

dance, has she? Look!'

He rose and pirouetted on his tail. The mud heaved itself into a great cloud. It began to glow with red.

Gwynion shot after Pangur, carrying Finnglas in his arms.

'Look after her well,' called Arthmael, revolving gracefully. 'What she needs is a square meal and an enemy to fight. See what you can find.'

'But aren't you coming?' squeaked Pangur. 'Quick!'

'You don't need me! The Pengoggen does. It must be very lonely for him down here.'

'*Lonely!*'

'Well, after he's eaten everyone, of course.'

'The blood from his wounds drifted down over five imprisoned sailors. They began to stir.

'But Niall . . . You've got to save Niall!'

'I have given you Finnglas, haven't I? What more do you want? She was dying for a fight.'

'You . . . *Miaow!*'

As the blood penetrated the cloud, the sea-bed flung itself upwards. Mud, pebbles, crabs, shot through the water in a furious tornado. Through the whirling fog two huge red eyes came hurtling towards them in a forest of waving tentacles. Gwynion, holding Finnglas like a baby, gave a great flick of his tail and streaked down the passage, with Pangur scrabbling desperately to keep up with him.

As the gulley began to climb, Pangur threw a last terrified look over his shoulder. Behind him he saw Arthmael leap in a great arch over the Pengoggen's head. Now he was circling, skipping, twisting, just out of reach of those lashing tentacles. In the red glare his blood flowed down and mingled with the dripping slime. Then the rocks hid him. Pangur's last glimpse was of the laughing dolphin dancing into the very jaws of death.

When the water grew lighter and clearer, and the sun came drifting down in golden threads, they stopped. Gwynion lowered Finnglas gently on to the sand. She cried out in agony as her feet touched the sea-bed and cramp seized her. They massaged her wasted limbs, while she made horrible faces of pain.

Pangur peered back, down the dark gulley through which they had escaped.

'I wish Arthmael would come. He's been a long time.'

Finnglas looked down at her nails in disbelief. Fragments of Arthmael's skin still clung to them.

'I wounded him. He came to save me, and I wounded him. He was bleeding when we left him.'

'He will not come,' Gwynion said sadly. 'The Pengoggen is death. Those who go to him never return.'

'No!' cried Pangur shocked. 'No! He is Arthmael, the Dancer!'

'Look at me. I went to the Pengoggen and I have come back,' protested Finnglas.

Gwynion shook his head.

'Only because he took your place.'

There was a long silence. The water crept coldly through Pangur's fur. Finnglas rose to her feet.

'We must go back and help him.'

Her hand went to her scabbard, and she started suddenly.

'No!' cried Gwynion and Pangur at the same time.

Gwynion grasped her arm with his cold, frightened fingers. 'You can't!'

'He wants you to save Niall; he told us so.' Pangur spoke rapidly.

'I did not come seeking Niall. What is Niall to me?'

'What were *you* to Arthmael?'

Pangur and Finnglas glared into each other's eyes, green into hazel. Then a flush mounted into Finnglas's pale face and she turned on her heel.

'I'm sorry,' muttered the princess for the first time in her life. 'Where is Niall?'

'On the dancing-floor of Ancofva. But you can't go there, Earthmaid!' Gwynion protested. 'The mermaids would kill you. You are the one who can break their spell, you see.'

'That is why I must go,' she told him proudly. 'If Arthmael can brave the Pengoggen for me, shall Finnglas be afraid to face mermaids?'

Pangur looked at her thoughtfully. Her chequered cloak was caked with mud. She looked pale and weary, and her hair still bore the traces of Arthmael's blood.

'Get her something to eat,' he said to Gwynion. 'She's going to need it.'

Gwynion brought her a handful of oysters and watched her sadly as she swallowed them.

'You do not know what you are doing.'

'Yes, I do.'

When she had eaten, she knotted her hair firmly behind her and pulled her muddy cloak straight.

'Now. Show me where Niall is.'

As the merman glided unwillingly forward through the pathways in the rocks, Pangur looked back longingly. The dark cleft behind him did not ripple with life. There was no silver belly, quivering with laughter, no dancing tail, no surge of joy.

'*Arthmael!*' whispered Pangur. 'Oh, come back, Arthmael, *please*!'

But the sea was silent. A terrible loneliness washed over him.

Under Gwynion's great shadow Finnglas swam purposefully, and the white cat struggled beneath them both. The rocks narrowed between sheer walls. A familiar curtain of sea-lettuce fluttered. Morwenna's chamber.

All at once, Pangur cried out, 'Listen, Finnglas! *Hide!*'

A stream of singing was rushing down the passage towards them. They dived through the curtain and listened, trembling, while Gwynion's great tail hung down and shielded the door. The music swept past and the sea grew still again. The evening sun fell softly from far above.

Finnglas stood looking down at the chamber, where she and Cruimthan had fought Morwenna and lost. There was no sign of that bitter struggle now. The shells had been raked into spiral patterns of mother-of-pearl. The sand had been brushed. She looked all round the empty floor and turned very pale. Then grimly she swam out through the curtain and followed Gwynion to the foot of the great stairs.

With a whispered word, Gwynion swam past them, up towards the surface. The merman sentries turned to greet him. Finnglas and Pangur climbed softly up the stairs and stole behind them.

The dancing-floor of the mermaids was golden with reflected light. The sky glowed rose through the waves above their heads. Fronds of green sea-lettuce swayed to their song. And the mermaids were dancing. Weaving their opal-hued tails in ribbons of colour. Sky-blue twining through pink, saffron with leaf-green, violet shimmering round a sheath of silver. Twisting, fanning, gliding, rising, while they sang to harps of narwhal and horns of ivory.

At the slow-spinning centre of their wreathing colours swayed a tall flame of red. Rose-red, blood-red. Beautiful, ancient, terrible. The grey-haired Sea Witch was leading the mermaids' dance. More awful in motion, like a hunting shark.

Finnglas stood on the topmost step. She did not seem afraid. She looked like a dirty boy, come in from hunting. For a moment, the mermaids did not notice her. The bewitched prisoners had not seen her. They lolled against the rocks, smiling broadly, mesmerized, drunk with the beauty spiralling all around and above them. To one side sat Niall, watching through half-closed eyes as Morwenna danced over him.

Pangur crouched down as small as possible, feeling his

terrified glance dragged back to the Sea Witch. Beside him Finnglas drew herself up straight and called in a voice like a hunting horn, '*Niall!*'

Pangur hid his eyes behind his paws.

The music broke off like shattered crystal. In the sudden silence the Sea Witch spun round to face them, reared like a waking serpent. Pangur willed himself not to look. He was seized with a terrible urge to dive back down the steps. *Now*, before it was too late.

But Niall did not move. Morwenna came skimming down in a shimmer of azure to hover over the young monk. Her hands closed about his shoulders, protective, angry.

'Do not listen!'

'Niall! Look at me!' Finnglas's command rang out.

The Sea Witch's fins began to lash. She leaned forward. Her grey hair floated out from her shoulders like an encroaching fog. Through it, her green eyes glared at Finnglas. Her voice boomed like breakers against the cliff.

'WHO DARES TO NAME MY CAPTIVE?'

'Don't look at her!' cried Pangur.

'WHO HAS ENTERED ANCOFVA WITHOUT OUR CALLING? APPROACH ME, BOY!'

'Finnglas, don't look into her eyes!'

Morwenna shrieked, 'Finnglas! That is no boy! It is the *Earthmaid!*'

The Sea Witch's finger shot out like a stabbing spear. 'KILL HER!'

The shoal of mermaids massed and drove towards Finnglas. They were silent now. White, set faces, golden hair, tails stiff in a rainbow phalanx. Their finger-nails were curved like claws, their sharp fins spread to strike. Finnglas's hand flew uselessly to her side.

'Your sword!' Pangur wailed suddenly. 'I knew there was something different about you, Finnglas! You've lost Cruimthan!'

The mermaids were circling madly round Finnglas, hissing 'Earthmaid!' Yet still they seemed afraid to close in and strike.

'Niall!' yelled Finnglas. 'Wake up, Niall!'

'SILENCE HER!' sang the Sea Witch.

Morwenna's white hand shot out, clawing at Finnglas's face. The girl clenched her fists and struck back, brown knuckles bruising white flesh.

One of the mermaids gave a sudden tinkle of laughter, like a silver goblet falling.

'Is that a woman? *That,* an Earthmaid?'

Now mocking laughter shivered round the spinning circle. Like tiny fragments of glass. Jagged. Dangerous.

Pangur cried, 'Quick, Finnglas! Run! They're not afraid of you any more!'

But the mermaids' nails were poised in front of them, their sea-green eyes glittering for the kill. There was no way out. They drew a deep, singing breath together and flung themselves forward.

The sea-bed heaved beneath them. Sand and shells exploded upwards in a blinding, stinging fog. Great boulders staggered with the shock. The mermaids screamed.

Above their cries, the Sea Witch trumpeted, 'THE PENGOGGEN STRIKES!'

'Arthmael!' shrieked Pangur.

The sand began to settle. The foam-white, frightened faces of the mermaids appeared. All the men were on their feet now, looking round them in confusion. Last of all, like a late, storm-filled dawn, the Sea Witch emerged out of the murk, standing wild-eyed before her amethyst throne. She levelled her arm at Finnglas and howled, 'FINISH HER NOW!'

The mermaids gathered themselves. For the last time Finnglas's hand went to the empty scabbard.

'Not that, Finnglas!' cried Pangur desperately. 'It's not men they're frightened of. Be what you are. Be a woman! Oh, where is Arthmael?'

For an agonized moment, Finnglas hesitated. Then, as the mermaids sprang, her hands went up to her head and in a flash she had loosed the knot of her hair. The long brown curls that Arthmael had freed tumbled down over her shoulders. She snatched the cloak from her neck and tied it flowing round her waist like a kirtle. Her white throat, collared with gold, sprang free from her tunic. And the men stared at her.

'I had a wife, and nine fine sons and daughters,' one of them said wonderingly.

'My Jenifer! I was on my way to be married.'

'I have left my wife alone to work the farm!'

And suddenly they were running towards her.

The furious mermaids swooped down. Finnglas ducked, twisting, beneath their sharp fins and ran forward. Niall was staggering to his feet.

'Finnglas? Martin's sister?' he said stumblingly.

'Yes! Run! Oh, come on, you stupid monk!'

She seized him by the hand and pulled him after her. All the men were running now. Sailors, merchants, warriors. Pangur came skittering through their legs. The mermaids were turning.

'Run! Swim! Fly for your lives!' cried Finnglas.

'No, Niall!' Morwenna shrieked. 'Stay with us!'

The Sea Witch mounted her throne like fire through charcoal. The mermaids were streaking after their fleeing prisoners.

'FOOLS!' she called. 'SING TO THEM!'

Like a flight of arrows, the shafts of song came piercingly behind them. The sea rocked with magic.

'Stop your ears,' cried Finnglas. 'Follow me!'

She was soaring towards the air, still hauling Niall by the hand. The men came rushing after her, fighting the clutching mermaids off, leaving shreds of clothing in their sharp white fingers. Up and up. Following the girl Finnglas to the earth and the sky.

'SING!' clamoured the Sea Witch. 'SING THE GREAT SPELL-SONG!'

The music of their calling broke like a choir of angels. Wondrous, magical, compelling. But the men's fingers were in their ears and their thoughts were in their eyes, following after Finnglas. The sea broke into hummocks as they surfaced. Hundreds of heads and shoulders, like a pack of seals. Prisoners, marvelling in the daylight they had forgotten.

'Don't stop! On, to the shore!' Finnglas yelled to them.

The calling was gaining on her, like the baying of the hounds of heaven. Some of the men were beginning to turn.

'Keep your ears shut!' roared Niall, fully awake now, and stuffing his fingers in his own. 'Make for the land! Follow Finnglas!'

Struggling, kicking, they urged their bodies shorewards. The mermaids burst from the sea behind them, like flowers opening in the sun, like irridescent mackerel, and singing, singing as though their silver hearts were bells. The sun stroked their shining tresses and their voices chimed across the water to the men. Finnglas was standing on the beach, calling to the prisoners. They could not hear her, with their fingers tight in their ears. But they saw the white gleam of her shoulders and her curling hair falling to her waist, and they thought of home. Their thrashing feet found shingle at last, and they waded, staggered, panted up the beach to safety.

And behind them all surfaced a weary, white cat, paddling the waves with tired and tiny paws.

'Niall! Follow! Niall! Come back to me!'

Morwenna threw out her white arms pleadingly. Her song of grief keened to the fading sky.

But Finnglas tore a handful of wool from the monk's robe and stuffed it into his ears.

The light was dying. The sea wept, as the mermaids of Ancofva mourned their great loss. The pale, round moon lifted above the ocean. Finnglas shuddered.

Wailing, Morwenna turned and saw the struggling Pangur. A smile of triumph lit her ice-green eyes.

18

The rescued prisoners crowded round Finnglas, jostling each other for a sight of the girl who had saved them.

'The blessings of heaven upon you, lady.'

'May the milk of your cows run always sweet, and the corn grow springing where your feet have passed and the hands of angels smooth the pillow where you sleep.'

'Will you stay with us now and be our queen?'

Finnglas frowned and pushed them aside. She unbuckled the useless scabbard and looked round the beach.

'Where is Pangur?' she said suddenly.

Pangur gasped as a buffeting breaker rolled over him. Here on the surface, the waves had the grip of winter, and the air struck chill. He lifted his head with difficulty and his blurred eyes found the dark line of hills. Pale patches of snow gleamed under their crags.

Another icy wave took his breath away. When he looked again, the beach was far, far out of reach. The faint songs of the mermaids were like the buzzing of grasshoppers in his failing ears. One by one they ceased, as the mermaids slipped below the waves, down to their empty halls. Between him and the shore rolled a vast grey sea. With paws feebly moving he watched it grow wider and wider. The chill entered his heart as he knew that the tide was carrying him out to sea.

A climbing breaker blotted the hills from his sight.

'Help!' gasped Pangur. 'Somebody help me!'

His sodden fur was growing heavier. His aching limbs were barely moving now.

'Help!' he choked.

'Ssh!' hissed the breakers, smothering his face with foam.

He felt himself sinking. The magic had gone from the water. The sea would not hold him now.

'Arthmael! Help me!'

'Hold on!' a brave voice cried.

He opened his eyes with a start. It was not Arthmael's call. He saw the pale, determined face of Finnglas cresting the waves towards him. Her thin brown arms beat the water into spray. Her hands reached out and grasped him.

'Finnglas!' he said in a shaking voice, burying his claws in her tunic. 'I couldn't swim. I was drowning!'

'Did you think I would let you go, after you brought Arthmael to save me? Dishonour to me if I let you sink as I left Melisant.'

She gripped him firmly and struck out for the shore.

After a while she said in a low voice, 'Pangur. The land's not getting any nearer. The tide is running stronger than I can swim.'

'Let me go,' begged Pangur. 'Save yourself.'

'Never!'

She struggled on, but the distant hills grew lower and lower.

'It's no good, Pangur.'

'Arthmael? Oh, where is Arthmael?' whispered Pangur. 'Why doesn't he come?'

A dark-sided wave, higher than all the rest, climbed before their eyes. And up through its glassy walls rose a violet shadow. The spray broke in the rising moonlight and the crest of the wave-top streamed with silvered hair. Morwenna reared above them. Her eyes glinted wickedly as she called down.

'So! This time, Morwenna wins!'

'Oh, no, she doesn't!'

The great, wool-clad shoulders of Niall thrust through the wave behind her. Morwenna threw back her head and lifted her face to the moon. The night shivered with her laughter.

'You would not follow for love of me. But I knew that for them you would come! Now, I have you.'

Her eyes grew wide with desire.

'I'm sorry, Morwenna,' Niall told her. 'But I'm a monk. I have forsworn the love of women . . . and of mermaids.'

'It's a pity you didn't remember that sooner,' muttered Pangur ungratefully.

Niall ignored him. He tucked the exhausted cat into his cowl. His hand reached out and grasped Finnglas.

Morwenna came streaming down the wave towards him. Her arms stretched out imploringly. Her throat began to swell with music.

'Oh, not now, Morwenna,' said Niall. 'It's been a hard day.'

Diving through the wave, he thrust for the shore.

Morwenna spun round. She saw Niall's hand clasped round the weary Finnglas. In a jealous fury she mounted a cresting wave.

'Niall!' cried Pangur. 'Beware Morwenna!'

The spell rang out across the darkening water, soared to the climbing moon, trawled the vast ocean with the great calling-song of power.

Pangur twisted his head the other way.

'Look out!' he called suddenly. 'What's that?'

A skein of lights was driving at them out of the darkness. Lights glowing on sail, lights riding the bows, lights flooding from the cabin. All the lights of a long, fierce, sharp-prowed warship, with space for many warriors and weapons.

For a moment they marvelled at it. Then the sea rose on the other side of them in a commotion. An angry, cresting wave seared past the swimmers, heading across the intervening sea towards the ship. Morwenna, hair streaming gold in the lantern light, a flicker of blue lightning in the depths, a storm of baffled desire.

And singing as she came. Singing to the stars above the clouds. Singing down magic from the moon. The silver song of her calling. Flinging the net of her music, as she wove it, over the ship, like a skilled fisherman with a great salmon. Trapping, binding, compelling, hauling it in. The ship turned towards her like a well-schooled horse, galloping to her bidding.

She swam back fast. Hiding behind Niall and Finnglas.

And still she sang. Pure, sparkling music, with all the beauty of her love for Niall. With all her urgent hate of Finnglas she sang. And still the ship came sweeping on. They could see men crowding the bows in the darkness. Straining forward for a sight of her who sang to them. She darted out. Lovely in the moonlight. And back again. The bows of the vessel drove straight towards the swimmers.

Niall roared. 'Stop! Bear away! For God's sake, turn!'

But above his voice Morwenna filled the night with music. The white bow-wave was rushing nearer.

'She'll sail right over us! They haven't seen us! Stop, you fools!'

Finnglas tried desperately to swim out of the way. The ship crested the last black-sided wave and towered over them.

'Arthmael! Save us!' screamed Pangur, as they wallowed helplessly in the trough beneath.

The crest of the breaker curled and the creaming foam began to run. Morwenna's voice rose in the last bell-like chime that would kill them all. Then, as the bows tilted, her song broke off suddenly in a high, keening lament, an agony of remorse.

'*No, Niall!* Don't die! Forgive me!'

The sharp wail rang to the stars as though her heart would break ... then it quavered, giggled, and burst into uncontrollable laughter.

'Stop it!' she cried to someone. 'You're tickling me! *Stop* it!'

The ship swooped down. There were frantic shouts of alarm. Released from the spell, men heaved at tiller and oars, wrestling the sail around. A surging wave picked up the swimmers and scraped them bruisingly along the warship's side. The wake seethed past, the swell heaved beneath them, the ship rolled aside.

Niall and Finnglas clung to each other. Morwenna was writhing helplessly in the water. In vain she struggled to dodge some underwater commotion that pursued her.

'Go *away*! Don't *do* that! I can't stand it!' Fury and laughter were battling in her voice.

A shining face popped to the surface, rolled a round,

bright eye at all of them, and vanished. A dark shape leaped from the water in a double somersault.

'Arthmael!' shouted Finnglas and Pangur together. 'It's Arthmael! He's come back!'

Morwenna shot gasping to the surface, chased by the dolphin.

'*That?*' asked Niall doubtfully, taking the wet wool from his ears. '*That's* Arthmael?'

'Oh, yes!' Finnglas reached out her arms to him in delight. 'He's here!'

'He's escaped from the Pengoggen,' cried Pangur. 'He's safe!'

'Safe?' quavered Niall, as Arthmael dived, and showers of spray flew over them.

The dolphin powered from the water, arching across the stars. Finnglas gasped. A great, fresh scar puckered his side from throat to tail. He dived again, drenching them with foam. Then his wet beak rose and nudged Finnglas's face gently, wiping away the tears of joy from her cheeks.

'Silly Finnglas. Did you think you could get rid of me as easily as that?'

'But it's been so long. And you didn't come.' Her fingertips reached out. Fearfully they traced the long, unhealed scar. 'Did *I* do *that?*'

The bright eyes teased her. 'Well, not *all* of it! But for your sake it was done.'

Then he butted Morwenna's ribs with his bulbous nose. She flashed away, but quicker than her, he charged. His tail swept round and flicked her into the air. She shrieked. Pangur remembered that feeling. Dropping out of the sky. Leaving his stomach behind. The grinning jaws below. Arthmael caught her on his nose and balanced her there while she screamed again. Then he dropped her, splash, spreadeagled, undignified in the water, and tickled her under the arms till she begged for mercy.

'Stop it! Stop it!' gasped Morwenna.

'Do you still feel like singing? Won't you sing for me?'

'How can I? You know I can't!' she panted, furious.

'What a pity! Then I shall have to sing to you. Have you

95

heard me sing?'

He lifted his clown's face to the sky and shut his eyes. His blowhole opened in a funnel and a wobbling whistle wavered ridiculously into the night. Morwenna stuffed her fingers into her ears. Arthmael's flippers smacked them away. He bent his head and whistled into her ear, off-key. Her lips began to twitch.

'There! I told you, didn't I? You can sing better than that. Come on, Morwenna. Do what you were made to do. Sing my song.'

She shook her head. But all the time his flippers were herding her away before him. The climbing rollers hid the pair from view.

'Arthmael!' cried Pangur suddenly. 'Don't leave us!'

The dolphin's head popped out from the crest of a wave.

'I will always answer when you call me, little Pangur. To the end of my days.'

They listened through the darkness to the faint splashing. Presently there came a startled cry from Morwenna. Next, she laughed. Her voice rose in a breathless snatch of song. Silence followed. Then, further off, Arthmael's whistle joined her in a broken refrain. Distant now, a weaving strand of music. Arthmael shrill, laughable, tone-deaf, and Morwenna's voice singing now from her heart. The listeners lay silent in the water as the two voices rose together more surely, blended into one note, faded into the distance, still singing together. A last fluting chime shivered across the sea like a gust of laughter. And all was still.

'Well,' shouted a rough voice above them. 'Do you want to be rescued or don't you?'

They turned to find the warship looming over them. Its sails hung slack from the lowered crossyard, like a horse's head breathing after hard galloping. Curious faces peered over the gunwale.

Niall grasped the rope that girded the side.

'After you,' he said to Finnglas.

She swarmed aboard.

'A woman, is it?' Murmurs of surprise ran round the deck.

Then, 'Another of them!' as Niall clambered over in his dripping robe, with Pangur still hidden inside his cowl.

'No. Look at his shaven head. It's a monk!'

A growl from many throats made Pangur shiver.

'Brood of vipers.'

'We have no love of monks aboard this ship.'

'No matter,' said Niall stoutly. 'Just set me down on the nearest land. That's all I ask.'

'You keep bad company,' said the captain. 'Two devils of the sea that would have led us to our deaths.'

'Devils!' Finnglas's voice rang out in anger. 'Dare you speak so of Arthmael, that saved us from the Pengoggen and from you?'

'Aye. Fish-tailed devils. She that steals the men from Kernac's ships. And he that looses the catch from Kernac's nets.'

'Kernac!' Finnglas cried out. 'Is this ship *Kernac's*?'

'Aye. The winter king that rules the Summer Isle. And well the coasts of Erin have cause to know his name. For a twelvemonth now we have been his sword to spill their blood, his torch to burn their houses, his whip to drive their children into slavery. Bitter the day that saw the king's son murdered and his daughter drowned. But bitterer still the fate of those who did it.'

'No!' groaned Niall.

Pangur trembled in his hiding-place.

But Finnglas's eyes sparkled with fury.

'Then half that grief and half that rage were for nothing! Look well, men of Kernac. Finnglas, the king's daughter, is still alive!'

She stepped forward into the lantern light.

There was a gasp of wonder. A moment's silence fell over the ship. Then mocking laughter, cruel as hailstones, burst from fifty throats.

The captain stepped forward and struck her across the mouth.

'I swear by my father's grave that if she were alive to hear you say that, she'd split you from your skull to your toes, you impudent bitch! Finnglas, Kernac's daughter, in a slimy skirt? Did you never see the princess? Finnglas Red-Hand we called her, though not to her face. She was more a man than the king's own son that went for a monk. There were three things by which you would know her. She never moved outside Rath Daran without them. The royal brooch of garnets at her throat. Her long sword Cruimthan at her side. And between her knees the brave horse Melisant that could outrace the chariots of the wind. And you stand there, you mud-smirched trollop, with draggled skirt and unbound hair, and use the name of Finnglas, Kernac's daughter!'

The princess raised her head proudly.

'My brooch I gave to make a fishing hook. My sword was taken when I fought the mermaids. And Melisant ...' Her voice broke. She steadied it bravely. 'Melisant is lost. But I am still a princess. Down on your knees, you dogs of Kernac, that dare to strike the daughter of your king! Behold the collar of gold my father gave me!'

She pulled back the neck of her tunic. The red-gold torque gleamed around her white neck.

There was a murmur of fear. Then a voice shouted out of the darkness.

'Robber!'

'She found the princess's body on the rocks!'

'She hid it from the king and stole the gold!'

'Death to the thief!'

They rushed upon her.

'Don't touch her!' Niall lunged forward. Men seized him from every side and wrestled him back.

'Hullo! What's this?'

Rough hands clutched at his squirming cowl.

'What have we here?'

They had found Pangur's hiding-place. They unhooked his claws and pulled the trembling cat out. He was set down on the deck. There was a hiss of indrawn breath, then a cry of fury.

'The cat! The white cat! The Unlucky One!'

'A white cat and a monk! It's them! The murderers!'

The whole crew was yelling for blood.

'Kill them! Kill them!'

Knives flashed in every hand. Light glinted on sharp blades like the fangs of wolves. Pangur cowered on the deck as the ring closed in.

'Help!' he gasped.

Finnglas's voice rang out desperately.

'Hold, vile pigs of Kernac! On your knees! In the name of your king, I order you ... Oh!'

Her cry broke off as her feet shot from under her and she went flying through the air down the sloping deck. The terrified Pangur saw the ring of blades sparkle and scatter into pieces as Kernac's crew toppled in every direction, dropping their weapons. Niall fell with a thud and rolled slowly towards the gunwale.

But the gunwale was rising up to meet him now, and they were all slipping and tumbling the other way. The ship rolled like a playful whale, first one side and then the other.

Niall clutched at the mast as he slithered past. 'It must be Arthmael!' he gasped.

A beaming black face rose into the air above him.

'Well done, brave Niall, that found me last and understand me best. You are a wise fool who trusts the clown of God.'

99

A cloud of white spray rose to the moon as he fell back into the water. Then from the other side of the ship a second voice rang out in high, joyous laughter. The ship tilted that way.

'Morwenna?' gasped Finnglas and Niall, clinging on the climbing rail.

Arthmael leaped higher than the mast in a triple somersault.

'Yes, Morwenna!' he called down as he flashed over their heads.

He curved across the stars and dived on the other side. They heard the splash, and then twin peals of laughter. The deck dipped terrifyingly down, threatening to bury itself under the waves. High on the starboard rail two merry faces appeared, one white, one black. Together they rolled the ship the other way. Arthmael lay low in the water beneath them now. He stroked Morwenna's tail lovingly with his flippers and called up to them.

'She sings a song worth waiting for. The song I have hoped a thousand years to hear. The music she was always meant to make. The song of life. Listen well when Morwenna sings to you.'

Then he winked at the mermaid, and laughing at each other, they tipped the ship back again.

But as the deck levelled, Kernac's men were scrambling to their feet, hands grabbing at fallen weapons, feet finding a balance, eyes glinting furiously at the helpless three.

'Excuse me,' said Arthmael. 'I think it's time for ...'

His last words were drowned in a rush of wind. Fire streaked across the heavens as the cracking of ropes was swallowed in a roar of thunder. Even the lowered canvas could not withstand the gale. With a sickening change of motion, the ship shot forward out to sea.

20

The air was alive with the hideous lashing of ropes, like a nest of snakes. The unbound sail screamed and bellied, hurtling them forward at the mercy of the gale. Kernac's crew leaped for the writhing sheets, fighting to master the sail before it split or the mast snapped. Their captain battled with the steering oar, forcing the frightened ship to point downwind, to take the mountainous waves stern on, to bury herself under the black weight of water and throw it aside as she mounted the next crest.

'Bail, damn you!' he shouted, as soaked now as those he had rescued. 'Do you want us all to die?'

There were no hands to spare for knives now. Every man wrestled for the life of the ship, subduing the ropes, capturing the sail, reefing it to an arm's breadth of straining canvas, just enough to give steerage way to the helmsman. Finnglas and Niall, up to their waists, found buckets awash in the swilling well of the boat and raced the rollers to empty the ship before the next wave swamped her. It was panting, shivering, desperate work. No time to talk, and teeth chattering as the wind bit through sodden clothing to the bone.

For hours they fought, till arms grew heavy, and muscles burned, and the mind grew numbed and wished only for sleep, even for death. At the lowest hour, when the will to live is feeblest, they heard from the darkness round them, a grinding roar, like a ravening monster in its lair that scents the approach of an unwary stranger. Every movement was suddenly stilled. They were all listening, fearful. Pangur, wet through and exhausted, felt the last of his hope grow cold and die.

'We're finished,' he whispered. 'If that's what I think it is.'

'Rocks,' growled the captain at the helm. 'But where?'

His hands faltered on the steering-oar and the ship heeled suddenly, broaching to the unpitying crash of the breakers. They were being rolled sideways and under. Amid yells of fear they fought to right and straighten her.

The menace was coming at them from every side. The sharp-toothed beast in the sea was raging at them, louder than the thunder, deeper than the screaming gale. White spray, visible even in the moon-shuttered darkness, flew past them. A wall of water rose in front of them, hung for a moment and fell with a crash, pounding itself into splinters of foam on the rocks.

'We're going to hit!'

'She's going under!'

'Abandon ship!'

Shadows of men went swooping overboard, like bats from a hollow tree in a cloud of darkness.

'You'll drown in this sea! Stay with the ship. I command you, stay!' Finnglas yelled.

But the steering oar, unmanned, swung over and the ship was tilting. The ropes, released, smacked against the deck. They were alone. Niall sprang for the helm and struggled to steady it. Finnglas grabbed at the sheets.

But Pangur had been swept up in the rush of movement. He hung tottering on the gunwale, afraid at the last moment of the black depths beneath him. He was hardly visible. One still white speck among the flying spume.

'Help!' he whispered.

And Finnglas saw him.

'Pangur!' she cried. 'Don't jump!'

'Wait!' roared Niall. 'Listen!'

Out of the storm a new sound was rising. A clear chime, mounting to the hidden stars. A song of hope out of a night of fear. A song of love in an ocean of loneliness.

'Follow me, follow me!' sang the voice.

Niall cried, 'It's Morwenna! Arthmael has sent her to guide us!'

He heaved at the helm, straining to turn the ship towards her voice. Finnglas ran to help him.

'Is it too late?' she panted. 'Will she answer the helm in such a sea?'

Pangur gripped the gunwale and screamed above the gale.

'Beware Morwenna! Don't trust her, Niall! She will lead us all to our deaths!'

The ship was turning away from the rocks.

'Follow me, follow me!' sang Morwenna, and the lightest tremble of laughter shook her voice.

The sea howled round them as they laboured across the waves. There were no hands to bail now, and the ship was filling. Then the song chimed clearly in front of them as the wind fell suddenly. Next moment, the storm bellowed again, then died to a whisper.

Finnglas licked her lips, watching the sail billow and empty.

'We are sailing between rocks again.'

There were thundering breakers on every side now. No light to steer by. Only Morwenna's song, like a silver chain, drawing them on.

'Look!' hissed Pangur suddenly. 'There she is, in the water!'

For the first time they caught the flicker of her phosphorescent tail. Its blue sheen led them into a narrowing gap. Breakers towered on either side. The gale buffeted them. The current was dragging them sideways.

'I can't hold her!' cried Niall. 'She's going on the rocks!'

'I said we should never trust Morwenna!' Pangur howled. 'It's too late now. She's done for us!'

Finnglas threw her strength beside Niall. Panting, they wrestled for their lives. And all the time, the mermaid's song was pouring skywards.

It broke off suddenly. There was a long, tearing wail of pain that hurt the heart to listen to. Even the wind fell silent to hear it. When it died, an awful stillness hung over the sea. There was only the muffled roar of the storm behind them.

'What's happened?' cried Niall fearfully, dropping the helm. He ran to peer over the side. 'What's happened to Morwenna? Who will guide us now?'

The boat rocked gently in the ripples from the storm. Finnglas lowered the barely trembling sail. She dropped the anchor overboard.

'Don't you see?' she said in a shaking voice. 'Can't you feel it? We are in harbour. Morwenna has brought us to safety.'

And she burst into tears.

21

'There she is,' said Niall. 'Lend me your cloak, Finnglas.'

Low in the water was a dull blue glow. It hardly flickered with life.

Finnglas and Niall lowered the cloak like a net and scooped the exhausted mermaid into its folds. She did not stir. As the clouds turned back from the setting moon they saw that her eyes were closed and her arms were streaked with blood.

'Pangur Bán.'

A stern voice spoke in the darkness.

On small, unwilling paws the little white cat picked his way to the bows and peered over.

'Arthmael?' he quavered.

'Of course, Arthmael.'

He glided under the wounded mermaid's side and laid her limp white arm across his neck.

'Look well on Morwenna, Pangur Bán. You did her great wrong. She risked her life to save you.'

'I'm sorry. I didn't know. I thought ...'

'How many times must blood be shed before you learn to trust me?'

'But I do! I *do* trust you!'

Arthmael gazed up at him. His face was silvered, sorrowful, as Pangur had never seen him look before.

'Learn, Pangur Bán, that I will always come when you need me. Though you, of all creatures, will wish you had never called.'

Then, clicking strangely, he sank beneath the waves, bearing Morwenna with him.

'What did he mean?' asked Pangur fearfully. 'What's going to happen?'

'I don't know,' said Niall. 'But we're safe now, and dawn is coming.'

They sat, huddled in wet boat cloaks, as the darkness stole homewards and the sky woke slowly into grey. A line of cliffs began to appear above the harbour. Pangur stared up at it. The river valley cutting through the rock. The shelving ledges. And at the top, a chapel and a cross. A low growl rose from his throat, a howl of longing.

'What's the matter, Pangur?' Niall reached out a sleepy hand to stroke him.

'I don't know. It can't be ... Niall, we've come *home*!'

'Home!' The boat rocked violently as Niall turned.

'The same beach! The same cliffs! The cross!' He rubbed his eyes wonderingly.

Light was fingering the ledges where the white buildings had sheltered like nesting gulls. There were black smudges in the hollows that the daylight did not seem to touch.

'Drusticc!' Niall's cry went echoing round the rocks. He was splashing overboard. 'It's me, Niall! I'm back!'

His shout came back to him from the cliffs, unanswered.

'Donal! Ita!'

Niall and Pangur were leaping ashore, running up over the beach, climbing the cliff path. They did not turn to see if Finnglas was following.

On board the ship Kernac's daughter looked up at the ledges. Then she picked up a fallen knife, stared at it, and let it drop again. More slowly she followed after Niall and Pangur.

They had reached the first ledge. They both stopped short. The library was a heap of blackened stones. Inside, the soft grey ash of thatch and books, trapped by the wind and flattened by the rain. The smell of stale soot rose under Finnglas's boot.

Niall buried his face in his hands and groaned aloud. Finnglas was white. Pangur cowered, too dumb to speak.

'Drusticc!' called Niall. '*Drusticc, where are you?*'

Up to the next ledge, and the charred refectory.

'Drusticc!' shouted Niall. 'Brogan! Maeve!'

Running now, past the ruined school. Past the burnt

106

cells of nuns and monks. Nearing the cliff-top.

'Drusticc!'

An inhuman screech stopped them in their tracks.

'Niall and Pangur Bán!'

They whirled round. High on the rocks above them crouched a weird figure. Hair long and tangled in the wind, beard matted, his body half-naked in tatters of brown wool. His eyes glared at them, and a jagged stone quivered in his hand.

'Have you not done enough harm to us all? Do you come back to haunt us now?'

'Who are you?' Niall asked in a hoarse voice. 'You know our names.'

But memory was stirring in Pangur's mind. A shaking hand. A pot of sheep's grease smacking into the sand.

'Enoch!' he cried. 'The convent fisherman!'

'Yes, Pangur Bán. Enoch! You stole my curragh and left me to Kernac's warriors.'

The stone struck the wall behind Pangur. He leaped aside.

'Wait!' shouted Niall. 'We have done penance for it . . .'

A second stone flew past his shoulder. They backed away hastily, up to the grassy cliff-top.

'Enoch!' begged Niall. 'For the love of God, tell us. *What has happened to the others?*'

For answer, a wild howl rose from Enoch's throat. It echoed desolately around the cliff-top. There was a moment's silence. Only the wind flattening the grass. Pangur crept closer to Niall. Then it seemed as though every boulder and tree began to move. Out from their shadows a fearful band began to creep into the daylight. White-haired and hollow cheeked, all dressed in rags. The remnant Kernac had spared from village and convent. They gathered in a hostile, staring ring. Enoch's trembling finger stabbed at the three.

'If you would have vengeance, behold the murdering monk and the unlucky cat that brought the curse of Kernac on our land. Because of them he burned your homes and took your children and razed our convent to the ground. What shall we do with them?'

107

A hiss of anger shivered on the wind. Pangur shuddered. The ring of frightened faces was edging closer. Hands shook as they reached out for sticks and stones.

'What is your will?'

'Death!' shouted a woman. 'They have deserved to die!'

And with a yell of hatred, the crowd rushed forward.

'Hold!' Finnglas cried desperately, hurling herself in front of Niall and Pangur. 'It was Kernac the king who has done this to you. Then let your vengeance fall on Kernac's daughter!'

A stone whistled through the air. Finnglas pitched forward, blood running from the side of her head. Niall gathered her unconscious form in his arms and started to run. The crowd were howling for blood. Stones pelted round them.

'To the beach!' shouted Niall to Pangur.

Finnglas opened her eyes and struggled with the monk.

'Put me down! A princess does not run away. It is dishonour!'

'It's common sense!' panted Niall. 'We've got to get to the ship!'

He held her by the hand now, dragging her over the grass. They were racing across the cliff-top. The sea was on one side, a sheer drop below. Behind them the screams of the crowd battered their ears.

In front of them the ground was falling. The river valley carved its way through the cliffs. The banks were dropping steeper and steeper. They were tumbling down them too fast to stop. A streak of bright water. A white beach. A glimpse of the ship.

The crowd bayed suddenly louder as they poured over the lip of the valley. Niall was in front, flying with long strides, with Finnglas hurtling after him. Pangur bounded after them on short white legs, desperately trying to close the gap between them. The flash of water grew brighter and brighter. A leaping commotion at the river mouth. A salmon net had been strung between rowan trees.

Stones thudded into the ground beside Pangur. Niall

had almost reached the sand. He and Finnglas were plough-ing across it. Pangur heard him shout.

'The ship! Kernac's men! *Run*, Finnglas!'

Then sudden pain. A blow struck Pangur full in the ribs. It knocked the breath from his body. It swept his feet from the hillside. The world was a black tumbling nightmare as he flew through the air. He waited for the rocks to crush him as he fell.

An ice-cold shock. Water closed over his head. He sank like a stone to the bottom of the river.

Choking, he fought his way back to the surface. The crowd were thundering down the slope towards him. His face rose spluttering to the light. Pain tore at his hind leg. He struggled to get free. It was dragging him back and under.

With a cry of terror he wrenched at his leg again, blind to the pain. He could not move. He was trapped in the salmon net.

Now his front paw was caught as well. The crowd was pounding past him on the bank. He was being sucked under, snarled in the fish trap, with the ice-cold water bubbling into his ears.

'Help!' he gasped.

More men were pouring over the rocks at the other end of the beach. Weapons flashed in the sunlight. Out of the sea came the dripping survivors of Kernac's crew, racing over the sand to their stolen ship.

Niall had reached the tideline. He was splashing through the shallow water towards the ship.

'Faster!' he urged Finnglas.

The crowd roared with fury as they burst out on to the beach. Stones churned the water.

'Help!' choked Pangur, as the river closed over his head. 'Somebody help me!'

Niall grasped the ship. Finnglas scrambled aboard. The monk sprang after her, dragging the anchor with him. He seized the oars and drove the ship into deeper water. With a yell of rage the warriors hurled themselves into the waves. Finnglas sent the sail climbing the mast. The ship scudded across the bay.

'*Help!*' screamed Pangur. 'Don't leave me to drown!'

And the very last woman at the back of the crowd heard him.

She turned and ran back to the river-bank, peering over. Her shout of triumph went ringing over the beach.

'The white cat! The Unlucky One! He's here! We've got him!'

The crowd's anger turned from the sea. They came surging back towards the salmon net, hatred in their faces. They had sticks raised in their hands. Stones seized from the beach.

'Kill him! Kill him!'

'Help!' wailed Pangur in pure terror. '*Arthmael! Help me!*'

A great cloud darkened the sun.

Out of the indigo sea, like a bolt of lightning, a white wave-wash came streaking between the rocks, storming past the stolen ship, tossing the swimming warriors aside, furrowing the still water of the bay, charging towards the salmon-net and the snared Pangur.

He saw the blue-black snout rushing towards him. No laughter in the bottle-nosed face now. No twinkle in the round bright eye. A fierce, fixed, unswervable, unstoppable tempest of deliverance.

'Arthmael!' he cried. 'Arthmael! Save me!'

22

The jaws opened on the salmon-net, and the tempest broke.
The slow-slipping river was churned into a maelstrom. Teeth
snapping, spray flying, fins sweeping the net aside, fluked tail
lashing the water into fury.

'Arthmael! Oh, Arthmael!' cried Pangur, as he felt his
legs coming free.

But a yell broke from the crowd on the bank above
them.

'He's freeing the cat!'

'He's breaking the net!'

'Kill the sea-devil!'

Their raised clubs darkened the sky like a thundercloud, and fell. The dolphin's great head arched over the
little white cat, shielding him from the blows. Again and
again the sharp white teeth bit through the net. And still the
great tail thrashed the water into sheets of spray, blinding
their enemies. The blows rained sightlessly down into the
storm.

Kernac's warriors, robbed of their prey, came charging
back towards the river-mouth. Their swords were black
against the sky. The blizzard of white water was flecked with
pink. Beneath it, swift, desperate, grim as Pangur had never
seen him before, Arthmael's jaws bit and bit again in a race
against death.

'Kill the white cat! Kill the sea-devil! Kill them both!'

He could see nothing but Arthmael's white underbelly.
He was safe beneath it. Then the last strand parted from his
tangled paw and he felt the current take him.

He was drifting down Arthmael's side, past the long
scars of Finnglas's fingers, gathering speed, swept under the
huge black tail beating in a welter of water. A noose of rope

was caught between its flukes.

'Arthmael . . .'

'Go!' roared Arthmael, with his jaws full of net. 'Go, and be thankful!'

He was moving faster now, slipping, spinning down the stream. He was out in the open bay. He was swimming. He turned his head.

'Arthmael?'

He glimpsed a great fountain of spray in the river-mouth. Then the jade-green waves rose higher than his head, blossoming with bubbles of rose-red foam, as though the sun was setting.

'*Arthmael!*' called Pangur. But his thin wail rose and lost itself in the empty sky. He was alone.

'Pangur Bán!'

Hands scooped him from the water. With a gasp he opened his eyes and found himself on Niall's lap. He shook his wet fur and pressed against him, purring. But the monk's hands dropped away from him. He was staring at the shore. Finnglas had lowered the sail. She too was staring at the river-mouth. A terrible silence gripped the warship.

Across the beach the crowd was thickening every moment, black as swarming bees. On the river-bank, stones were flying, clubs rising and falling, swords lifting against the sky. Over and over again.

'Come on, Arthmael! Come on!' groaned Niall, his knuckles gripping white on the edge of the boat.

'We've got to help him!' Finnglas's voice was shrill with despair.

The river-mouth was a dense mass of wading bodies. Over their heads the fountain of spray sank lower. Niall hid his face in his hands and wept.

'We've got to go back and save him!' cried Finnglas. She grabbed the steering-oar.

Niall's hand closed over her wrist. He pointed down at the water.

'It's too late. We must save ourselves now. Look.'

The first pink flecks of foam were touching the ship, like chaffinch feathers. But out of the river a stronger stream was

113

flowing. Bright red, streaking the turquoise water like sunset at noon.

'They're *killing* him!' whispered Pangur unbelievingly. 'They're killing Arthmael!'

'He can't die!' shouted Finnglas. 'He saved us all! Arthmael *can't* die!'

But his blood was staining the bay like a funeral fire.

A savage shout of triumph rose from the shore.

'It is finished,' breathed Finnglas, wide-eyed.

'He was Arthmael, the Clown, the great Dancer,' muttered Niall. 'When he dies, the dance is over.'

He began to tremble. He heaved on the oars. White-faced, Finnglas sent the sail shivering up the mast again. The warship fled from the convent, like an eagle chased by sparrows.

The light faded from the sea. The sun went down. They were alone on a grey ocean, abandoned, silent with fear, and cold with despair.

23

The wind moaned in the shrouds and died away.

And out of the twilit water a voice rose laughingly. 'You've come back! Are you all safe? We heard Pangur call.'

'It's Morwenna,' whispered Finnglas. 'Who's going to tell her?'

The white face swam around to the other side of the ship.

'What's the matter? Pangur is with you, isn't he? Arthmael did rescue him? When we heard his cry, Arthmael went from me like a salmon to the spawning, like a flood through a dam, like a whale in the mating season. Where is he?'

No one answered.

'What's the matter with you all?' Her singing voice called up to them. 'Where's Arthmael?'

The waves seemed to lap against the side of the ship with a sound like thunder. The creaking of the rigging screamed aloud. Pangur crept away from the rail and hid from her.

And then she knew. The sky was rent in two by a terrible cry. Sharp-edged, jagged, cruel as an iceberg, the inhuman keening of the mermaid screamed through the air, freezing the hearts of the listeners, forcing them to stop their ears, turning the stars to ice and the waves to fangs, echoing down into the very depths of the ocean. Even the Pengoggen shuddered in his red-eyed nightmare under the sea-bed. Pangur could not stop himself trembling.

The keening died.

'Where is he now?' Her voice spoke strangely from the waves. Small, childish, lost.

Still no one spoke. They took their hands from their ears.

115

'Where have you laid him? Why didn't you bring him with you? Oh, where can I see his body?'

'We didn't . . .' Niall struggled to tell her. 'We couldn't. He was caught in a net. They were all around him. There were hundreds of them. With clubs and stones. We couldn't get near him, Morwenna!'

'You left Arthmael to die? You left him alone with his enemies!'

In a flash of phosphorescence Morwenna whirled round. Serpent-blue she streamed away underwater. The dark ocean swallowed her.

'She's right!' cried Finnglas with desperate eagerness. 'We've got to go back! If we could find his body! He might not be dead! There might be something we can do.'

The others stared at her.

Then, 'I'm with you,' said Niall, trying to sound braver than he felt.

'And I,' said Pangur Bán.

They stole into the bay by moonlight and crept into the river-mouth.

Arthmael lay where his executioners had left him. Only the torn net and the muddied water covered him. His teeth were closed in a grin of triumph on the last severed strand that had set Pangur free. But his great fluked tail lay deep underwater, bound, tangled in a snare of death. The strong, black tail of Arthmael that had danced across the waves of seven seas. Whose springing muscles had lifted his face clean out of the water, leaping to meet the sun.

No more leaping. No laughter now. The broad skull was smashed, the flesh pulped, one eye hung from its socket.

Morwenna lay stretched beside him in the water, endlessly, endlessly stroking the battered body, that could not feel the touch of her small white hand. Her hair fell over him, as she wiped the blood from his wounds. She lifted her face to them, and the moonlight caught the hot tears that were running down her cheeks, the first tears she had shed in a thousand years, as her mermaid's heart broke in a storm of grief.

'Help me!' she pleaded with them. 'Help me free his

116

body and carry it away.'

They wrestled with the net. Deep underwater they freed his tangled tail at last. They held their breath then, believing still that the flukes must rise to the surface and with a great flick of joy drench them all with the laughter of flying spray. But it did not move. The lifeless body lay heavily on the river-bed. Only the muddied water went slipping past their feet, dark in the moonlight.

They tried to move him. But their arms slid on the slippery, shattered hulk. There was nothing to hold. No strength of theirs could shift this weight of death. Arthmael would swim no more.

The moon sank lower. Dawn paled the sky. The grey sides of the dolphin rose clear of the water.

'The tide is falling,' said Finnglas quietly.

'It's almost daybreak,' Niall said.

The beach began to glimmer with the touch of the first spring morning. The ship stood dark on the widening white sand. And the river, that could no longer bear Arthmael, went slipping, slipping away from him down into the sea, leaving his body beached upon the mud.

'It's no good!' cried Finnglas. 'We can't move him! What shall we do?'

Niall was pushing the ship out into the water.

But Morwenna lay down beside Arthmael, her arms twined round his neck, her falling hair shielding his shattered head from the light of day. Her rainbow tail shimmered upon the mud.

An edge of gold crept along the hilltops. And as the dawn brightened across the sky, Morwenna lifted her head and began to sing.

'Oh, hush, Morwenna!' begged Finnglas. 'Hush! They'll hear you!'

Never before had such enchanted music blossomed from the sea into the dawn. She sang for Arthmael. Never for Niall had she sang such love. Not for the sailors following her spells. Even the music with which she led them through the storm had not drawn them with melody like this.

He did not hear her.

117

Petals of rose uncurled in the morning clouds. Niall and Finnglas rowed the boat out from the shore.

'Morwenna,' Niall called, low and urgent. 'The tide's going out. It's nearly sunrise.'

Still she sang.

She sang of life in the dead ears of Arthmael. She sang of love to the broken body at her side. She sang of grief as the sun rose and the year woke into springtime.

And from their hiding-places the villagers heard her.

They came stumbling out from the rocks. They looked around, and a fierce shout rose from them.

The ship was sailing fast out of the bay.

They were pouring down into the valley, seizing sticks and stones.

'Oh, no!' pleaded Finnglas, kneeling in the stern. 'No! Not Morwenna too!'

The ship shot past the rocks and round the headland. Still the song soared into the speedwell sky in farewell. They heard it break.

Pangur's claws gripped the gunwale.

'*Morwenna?*'

Three last notes chimed. And then there was only silence.

The colours faded from the sky. But the white sand was flushed with pink, like a second dawn. It mingled with the brown tide-mark of Arthmael's blood.

'Morwenna!' groaned Niall. 'Oh, Morwenna!'

24

'Where can I go?' asked Finnglas bitterly. 'I can never return to my father now.'

Three days had passed. She stood at the bows of Kernac's ship wrapped in her cloak. She lifted her grief-stained face to the sky and her voice rose in a keening lament.

'Ochone! Ochone!
  The joy is gone from the water.

The dancer is dead.
  Our love will leap no more upon the wavetops.
Where is laughter now?
  If there is dying like this in the springtime,
What will be done in the winter?
  How shall we bear it?

Ochone! Ochone!
  The joy is gone from the water.'

Niall shook his head in disbelief, still struggling to understand.

'But he was Arthmael, the Fool, the Clown! I thought he *couldn't* die.'

Only Pangur said nothing. He crouched under the thwart. He could not look at the others.

'I have killed the great Dancer,' he thought. 'I have no home now. Arthmael has taken the death that was meant for me.'

The ship did not seem to need a helmsman. It took its own way over the weeping ocean. Niall stared down at the curving wake.

'I hadn't noticed,' he said. 'The year has turned, and the

wind has changed. It is blowing us back to the shore.'

Soon a mist closed round them. The waves darkened, flattened, smoothed to an oily swell. Over their heads a gull called, with mocking laughter. Others echoed. The ship stole slowly forward.

'Listen,' said Finnglas presently. 'I think I can hear breakers.'

They were creeping into a wall of fog.

'Shall I run down the sail?' asked Niall.

The ship nosed forward through the rocks, like a lamb scenting its ewe. There was a shudder beneath them, and the bows were still.

'We've beached,' said Finnglas.

Out of the mist a white-robed figure walked down the shingle towards them and grasped the gunwale.

'Hm!' said Drusticc the Abbess. 'A year and a day. I wondered if you would find me.'

Niall scrambled ashore and fell on his knees before her.

'Drusticc! You escaped from Kernac! You're safe!'

'Escaped, is it?' she said grimly. 'That's not what I'd call it. Do you know where we are? When Kernac's men had punished my body enough, they set me here on this island of rock, without food, without shelter, without boat, and left me alone to watch my convent burn. *Safe*, you say! I'm heartily sick of the taste of limpets.'

'Drusticc! . . . I'm sorry!'

She looked past him as Finnglas jumped ashore. Then she lifted Pangur and set him down on the shingle, none too gently.

'So! I sent you out in a leather fishing boat, and you come back to me in Kernac's warship. Was Enoch's curragh not good enough for the likes of you?'

'Enoch's boat is wrecked,' said Niall humbly. 'I lost it following the mermaids.'

'We have lost everything we loved,' said Finnglas.

Drusticc looked up, shading her eyes. Above their heads the sky was already spring blue, wheeling with gulls. She listened to their cries and smiled more kindly.

'That's not what I hear. I hear of a journey to the utmost

120

isles to fetch the great dolphin. I hear of prisoners rescued from the mermaids, restored to homes and families. I hear of three friends, that once were enemies, yet risked their lives to save each other. And of a mermaid who sings the songs of life. This was well done.'

'But you don't know!' burst out Niall. 'You don't know what really happened!'

'I have lost Melisant.'

'I let myself be bewitched by mermaids.'

'And some of the prisoners were eaten by the Pengoggen.'

'And half Kernac's men were drowned in the storm.'

'And my father has burned the convent and sacked the village. Those that are left are turned to hatred.'

'And Morwenna is dead.'

But none of them could bring themselves to say the words that lay heaviest on all their hearts. One name they could not speak, because his loss was more than they could bear. Pangur crouched at Drusticc's feet on the damp seaweed and mewed piteously.

She picked him up and he buried his face in her robe.

'You don't know,' he wailed. 'You don't know the worst thing of all. It was my fault. *I have killed Arthmael!*'

He felt Drusticc tremble.

'He died to save me. *Me?* I wasn't worth it!'

'But to him you *are* worth it, Pangur Bán, because he loved you.'

'I'd do anything to bring him back. *Anything*. But there is nothing I can do, is there? It is all over.'

'No, Pangur Bán. There is nothing *you* can do.'

Her chest was quivering now. Over his head her voice broke into ringing laughter as she turned him round to face the world.

'Oh, Pangur Bán! Did you think you could silence the great Clown, the Dancer! Did you think your little sin could put out the light of the world? Will you look there!'

A single shaft of sunlight struck down through the mist. They saw no land but, where it touched the water, waves broke against a rock. Around it, a glittering circle began to

grow, brighter and brighter, till they could hardly bear to look at it. The surface splintered. A boy's face rose, laughing in the sun as he tossed the wet hair from his eyes. His thin arms struck out strongly, cleaving the sea in blinding showers of spray, breasting the dancing wave-crests, legs thrusting up foam behind him. He grasped the rock and hauled himself up on it. A young, slight boy in a monk's robe.

'Martin!' Finnglas's shriek of joy rang over the bay. 'My brother Martin!'

She was dashing into the sea, plunging through the waves towards him.

'*Wait!*' Drusticc's commanding shout stayed her thigh-deep. 'Wait, Finnglas! Not yet.'

Finnglas stared across the water with longing.

The boy sprang on his hands and turned a cartwheel in the sun for joy.

A second, golden head surfaced beside him. Shining hair fanned through the sparkle of wave-caps like an unloosed sheaf of corn. The mermaid swam in sun-drenched spirals, her violet tail shimmered through the jade-green water.

'*Morwenna!*' Niall whispered, starting forward.

'Stay, Niall!' Drusticc laid her hand upon his arm. 'Listen.'

Morwenna lifted her face. Her golden voice climbed to the echoing cliffs, to the sky, to the sun, chiming for joy around the circles of the unseen stars.

Now Drusticc's arms held Pangur more strongly, holding his face still pointing across the bay. The watchers held their breath.

The great, scarred dolphin leaped straight up out of the ocean. The swift, blue-black length of him arched across the sun. It gilded the yellow streak along his side, silvered his flashing belly, made diamonds of his laughing eyes. He dived with an almighty splash. The waves of his leaping washed over their feet. Then his strong tail lashed once, lifting his joyful face to the world again.

'Arthmael!'

Pangur squirmed to leap free, to run to him.

'Not yet!' Drusticc's command rang out for the third

time. 'Not yet.' Then, more gently, 'Wait, Pangur Bán. Your turn will come.'

And in the midst of the laughter and leaping, Arthmael sprang up on his tail and danced for them.

The sunshine was warm on their faces. Martin threw a handstand on the rock. Morwenna flashed her tail, tossing up clouds of spray as she swam in circles around Arthmael. And as she swam she threw back her hair and sang, pure happiness in every crystal note.

Then, for the last time, Arthmael leaped from under the sea. Powering up through all the layers of creation. Soaring on into the sky and the sun.

The watchers gazed upwards till their eyes were dazzled, and they had to blink and turn away. When they looked again, the mist had closed upon the bay.

But overhead the sun was strengthening. The line of cliffs stood out across the sky. As the mist sank lower, they saw the black scars of the convent on the ledges.

'A year and a day,' said Drusticc. 'And yet not one stone raised upon another.'

'This ship is yours,' Finnglas stepped forward. 'My father burned your convent. His daughter will take you back to build it again.'

Niall looked down at his hands. 'I would have killed Pangur for ruining a single page of my Gospel. Now all the books we had are burned. These hands are yours, Drusticc. To paint and copy until I have restored all we have lost.'

Drusticc lifted her eyebrows. 'It may be dangerous,' she warned them.

No one spoke, but Pangur sprang into the bows. The others scrambled after him. The ship slid out from the shore.

'Home,' said Drusticc.

'The joy has come back to the water!' sang Pangur Bán.

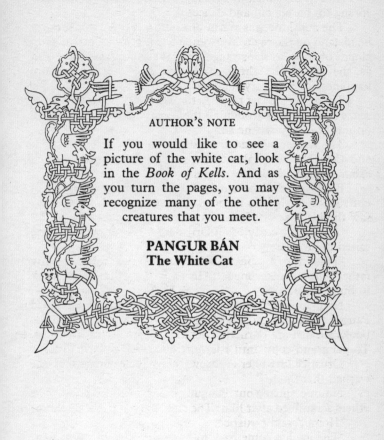

AUTHOR'S NOTE

If you would like to see a picture of the white cat, look in the *Book of Kells*. And as you turn the pages, you may recognize many of the other creatures that you meet.

PANGUR BÁN
The White Cat